The Moonlight Wedding

MARRIED IN MALIBU

BOOK 4

LUCY KEVIN

THE MOONLIGHT WEDDING

Married in Malibu, Book 4

Sign up for Lucy's Newsletter

lucykevin.com/newsletter

www.LucyKevin.com

Meg Ashworth has always lived her life by the book, until she finally breaks away from her family's strict rules to be a wedding designer at Married in Malibu. But she never expected that part of her job description would mean working day—and night—with one of the biggest rock stars on the planet.

Lucas Crosby desperately needs Meg's help to create a music video for his new single. She is so brilliant and beautiful that instead of hiring a model or actress to play the part of his true love in the video...he wants Meg! When their deep spark of connection grows far beyond their pretend relationship onscreen, can he convince her to take a chance on loving him in real life?

Chapter One

Meg Ashworth had been raised to be elegant and tidy, no matter the circumstances.

Yet here she was, running across the Married in Malibu parking lot, her silk dress, heels, hair, and makeup all destroyed by the rain pouring down. She hated being late to work, but it had taken her far longer than she'd anticipated to leave her mother's charity breakfast.

During the event, she had caught a glimpse of herself in the hall mirror and had been shocked by how much she looked like her mother, with her fussy hairstyle and the string of pearls around her neck. She certainly hadn't felt like *Meg*, as she was known to everyone at Married in Malibu, where she was in charge of designing celebrity weddings. No, this morning she had most definitely been *Margaret*.

Travis must have seen her on the security cameras, because the front door was wide open by the time she reached it. Meg was happy to see him smiling so often these days, thanks to his newly rekindled relationship with Amy, their on-staff portrait painter. Today, however, there seemed to be an extra quirk to his expression.

"Good morning, Meg. Rough traffic out there?"

"I had some things to take care of for my mother before coming in this morning." It sounded like she had been running errands for a doddering old woman who couldn't look after herself, rather than a society maven in peak health with an extensive staff. Meg looked down at her wet clothes in dismay. "If I'd known I was going to get caught in a downpour, I would have brought a change of clothes—or at least taken an umbrella with me. Sometimes it feels more like we live in Seattle than Malibu, doesn't it?"

"It sure does." He handed her one of the towels they kept on hand by the door to deal with unexpected showers. "But don't worry. Once you see who is in Liz's office, you're going to forget all about being dripping wet. I knew he was coming, of course, and yet I still can't believe it myself."

Travis had worked as a bodyguard to the A-list before taking this job, so he wasn't normally impressed by celebrities. What's more, this year they had already hosted weddings for several supermodels, world-renowned actors, and billionaires. Through all of it, Travis hadn't batted an eyelid. For him to be this impressed, the person waiting in their boss's office must really be special.

"Who is it?" There were several client meetings on the schedule for later in the week, but Meg couldn't remember seeing one on the calendar for today.

"You'll have to see for yourself," Travis replied, clearly relishing her anticipation. "Go on up as soon as you're ready. I believe they're waiting for you."

Meg did her best to towel off, then fix her hair and wipe away the mascara smudges under her eyes before making her way upstairs. She knocked on the half-open door.

"Come in."

The first thing she noticed was the star-struck expressions on her friends' faces. What celebrity could possibly have everyone who worked here so over the moon?

"Ah, here she is now, Lucas," Liz said. "The woman I'm positive will be the answer to your prayers."

Most celebrities looked less imposing and impressive in real life. Lucas Crosby, however, was utterly spellbinding. In well-worn jeans and a plaid long-sleeved shirt open over a Harley T-shirt, it was as though he'd just stepped off the cover of *Rolling Stone* magazine. He was tall and muscular, and his shoulder-length dark hair and dark stubble across his chin and jaw only served to highlight his masculinity. And his eyes were so starkly blue that she wondered if he wore tinted contact lenses.

Meg's feet started forward without any input from

her brain. The next thing she knew, they were facing each other in the middle of the crowded office.

"Hello." He leaned in close to shake her hand. "I'm Lucas Crosby."

Meg couldn't keep from laughing out loud at the thought that someone might not know who he was. How many of his albums had gone platinum? How many stadiums had he sold out in minutes? How many magazine covers had he been on? "Of course I know who you are."

She froze as soon as the words left her mouth. It wasn't the kind of thing she would normally say to a client. Thankfully, by the way his lips curved up slightly at the corners, he didn't seem to mind.

Hoping to give a more professional second impression, she held out her hand and said, "I'm Margaret Ashworth."

His hand over hers was strong and warm. "It's nice to meet you, Margaret." He was still holding on to her hand as he tilted his head slightly to one side and said, "I thought I heard Liz and the others refer to you as Meg, but I must have been mistaken."

"No, you weren't. My friends call me Meg."

"Can I call you Meg too?"

It was a simple question, and yet there was an intimacy behind his words that made her feel warm all over. "I'd like that."

She had never cared whether their clients used her nickname or not. But instinctively, she didn't want to be stuffy, fussy-haired, overly polite *Margaret* with Lucas Crosby. Just as she didn't want to let go of his hand when he smelled so good and his grip was so strong, yet comforting.

It wasn't until Liz cleared her throat that Meg finally remembered she and Lucas weren't alone. She jumped back as though he were fire and she polyester.

"Lucas, Meg is our brilliant designer I told you about. If anyone can design the perfect video shoot for you, it's Meg." Liz smiled at her. "Why don't you take Lucas through to your office so that you can talk over the details?"

Meg's legs felt like spaghetti as she led the way down the hall. Opening her office door, she winced at the fabric samples and drawings strewn everywhere.

"My studio looks a lot like this when I'm bringing a song to life," he said before she could apologize for the mess. "Just with more instruments and less fabric."

Relieved that he wasn't judging her, she gestured for him to take a seat before moving behind her desk. Her dress was still a little damp, but at least it wasn't sticking to her skin the way it had been when she'd first entered the building. "Liz told us a few weeks ago that you wanted to film a few scenes for your video here, but I didn't think it was on the calendar quite yet."

"My director, Seb, and I have spent the past two weeks working on this video for my new single. But nothing we've tried has worked. And then yesterday, the label called and said they want to move up the release date for the song." He ran a hand through his hair, obviously frustrated. "Since we were already planning to shoot a couple of scenes here next month, I called Liz last night and asked if we could shoot the whole thing here, instead. She was nice enough to slot me in immediately. And," he added with a smile so potent it nearly knocked the breath out of her lungs, "Liz has told me repeatedly how great your ideas are, so I can't wait to get started."

It was wonderful that Liz had so much faith in her. Her boss, and friend, had taken a chance on her when no one else would, and Meg couldn't stand the thought of letting her down.

Unfortunately, working on a music video wasn't close to anything she had done before. Sure, the idea sounded amazing, especially if it meant getting to spend time with Lucas Crosby. But she felt so far in over her head that she simply wasn't sure how it would work.

"I'm glad Liz was able to rearrange things for you. But..." She wanted to put this in the most diplomatic way possible. "Aren't most rock videos shot in dark alleys, or on mountain peaks, or in stadiums? I want to help you with it, but do you really think that I can transform a wedding venue into something suitable for your music?"

"I really do." Again, his smile was so gorgeous it nearly blew her heels right off her feet. "My song is called 'Perfect Moments.' It's about finding true love—and then doing whatever it takes to make sure that love lasts forever. Just like you guessed, our first attempts at the video were of me and my guitar on an empty stadium stage, and then in the desert lip-syncing the song as the sun rose behind me. This time around, I want to keep it simple and on point with a montage of a couple falling in love. The first time they lock eyes. Their first date. Their first kiss. And then saying *I do*."

Just that quickly, Meg's brain began to whir with the possibilities...even as it took more effort than it should have to stop imagining what it would be like to share a first kiss with Lucas.

"I love everything you've come up with," she said, "but what if, instead of the video ending at *I do*, we also show their first dance, and then cutting the cake together?" Before he could respond, another idea hit her. "And what if, for the very last scene, they head off into the sunset together in a convertible, with the bride's dress and hair flowing behind her as she tosses the bouquet? It could be the very last image on the screen—her beautiful wedding flowers flying up high into the sky."

"You're a genius." She could see the excitement on

his face. "It will mean so much more if we show that they're going to keep making these perfect moments together, even after the wedding." But then he frowned. "Honestly, at this point the only thing I'm worried about is finding the right person to play my bride. In order for this to work, there's got to be a connection between us on screen."

"How much time do we have to find locations, design and build sets—and find the perfect bride for you?" Honestly, Meg never thought she'd be offering to find *the perfect bride* for a client…

"After the issues I've had with making this video, and with the label pulling in the release date, we're down to a week."

"A week?" Trying to put together a wedding in such a short time was nearly impossible. But orchestrating her first-ever music video…?

It was downright nuts.

"What happens if you miss the deadline?"

"My record label is threatening to use the footage we already have." Lucas didn't look at all happy at the prospect.

"Okay." It was clear that she needed to make this happen for both Lucas and Married in Malibu. "In that case, it would be really helpful if you could play the song for me, so I know exactly what it is we're creating the backdrop for."

"I don't keep new songs on my phone anymore, since so many musicians have had their new music hacked off the cloud. But if you can find me a guitar, I'll play it for you live."

"We keep one of almost every instrument on hand just in case our wedding bands ever need a backup. Give me a minute, and I'll rustle one up."

She ran down the stairs, found a guitar in the storeroom, and was about to dash back up to her office when Jenn appeared holding two cupcakes.

"I was thinking you two might appreciate a sugar boost."

"This is great, Jenn." Meg had been so busy looking after her mother's guests at the charity breakfast that she hadn't had a chance to eat a bite herself. "Thank you."

But instead of simply handing her the cupcakes and heading back to the kitchen, Jenn looked down at the guitar in her hand. "Is he going to play for you?"

Meg nodded. "Hopefully, once I hear his new song, I'll be able to jump right into designing the scenes and sets for his video."

"On the one hand, I envy you for getting to work so closely with Lucas." Jenn gave a dreamy little sigh. "But on the other hand, none of us thought we'd ever be working on a music video. Are you okay with it? Because I know I'd be super nervous."

Even after working at Married in Malibu for several

months, Meg wasn't used to friendly concern. Her mother had always assumed any problem that didn't directly affect her wasn't worth concentrating on. And Meg's society acquaintances pounced on weakness, so it was best never to show any.

Well-brought-up young women didn't complain. They certainly didn't make things difficult for others.

"I can handle it," she assured Jenn with a smile. "Thanks again for the cupcakes. You're the best."

As she headed up the stairs to the office, she silently vowed that no matter the challenges she had to hurdle this week, somehow, some way, she would find it in herself to rise above them all.

Chapter Two

"Perfect Moments" didn't have the straight-ahead rock feel that the record label's marketing people insisted Lucas's fans wanted—and they weren't particularly happy about his going in a different direction with the video. Despite all that, however, Lucas felt excitement coursing through him.

He'd had a good feeling about Married in Malibu since his friend Jason Lomax had recommended the venue a while back. That feeling had only intensified once he'd met Meg. Lucas had always been one to trust his gut. His music was about speaking from the heart, and you couldn't do that if you ignored your instincts.

When Lucas's gaze had met Meg's for the first time, their connection had been intense. She'd seemed shy, even a little awkward around him. It was a nice change from the way women so often threw themselves at him, assuming he would be interested in a one-night stand simply because of what he did for a living. He'd long ago perfected the art of gently saying no.

Now, he couldn't escape the sense that he'd been waiting all this time for bright, beautiful Meg to come into his life and turn it right side up.

"Found one." She came back into the room with a beat-up acoustic guitar in one hand and a plate with two cupcakes in the other. "I hope it's okay that the guitar is a little rough looking. I tried to find a newer one, but this was the best I could come up with."

"This is my favorite kind of instrument—one that has obviously been played a lot and is a little rough around the edges, like me." There had been those in his career who had wanted him to clean up his look, to appear slicker than he was. He'd resisted. After all, if it was good enough for Springsteen…

"You don't look rough around the edges to me," Meg said, then seemed to catch herself. "That is, you're obviously hugely successful."

"I am now, but I wasn't exactly born to it."

She went still. "Do you think it's a bad thing when someone is?"

"Honestly, I think people should just be who they are and not worry about what anyone else thinks."

Meg stared at him for a few moments before finally nodding, then holding out the guitar. He was surprised to feel the burst of nerves as he checked the tuning. He didn't normally get nervous about playing a song for someone. He had literally millions of fans. He'd played stadiums around the globe. Singing one song for Meg so that she could help him plan the video shouldn't have felt like a big deal.

But it was. Because he *really* wanted Meg to like it.

He closed his eyes as he began to play. If he watched Meg watching him, he had a feeling he would never be able to get beyond the end of the first verse.

He gave the song his all, singing it with more emotion than he ever had before. Finally, with the last notes ringing out, he dared to open his eyes.

"It's *beautiful*," Meg whispered, looking incredibly moved. "I'm even sorrier now that I haven't listened to your songs before. I'm going to buy all of your albums tonight so that I don't mess this video up by not understanding exactly what you do."

"First of all, I'm not at all worried that you're going to mess something up," Lucas assured her. "And you should know that it actually means more to me that you like this song when you don't normally listen to my music."

"It's not that I've singled out *your* songs," she was quick to clarify. "I really haven't ever heard *any* rock music."

"What do you normally listen to?"

"Mostly classical. Baroque, pastoral, and opera, of course."

Lucas suspected that in the world Meg had grown up

in, opera probably merited that *of course.* Whereas he hadn't seen an opera until he was an adult, and even then, it had taken him years to understand it.

"Although," she added, "I've secretly always liked jazz. There are some jazzy influences in your song, aren't there?"

He was pleased that she had caught them. "Lately, I've been listening to Martin Taylor, Larry Carlton, Miles Davis."

"I love Miles Davis." She said it as though it was a guilty pleasure. "Now, since we don't have any time to waste, I hope it's all right with you if we start fleshing out our plans this morning."

"That's what I was hoping you'd say."

"Great." Her smile was so beautiful that his heartbeat kicked into overdrive. "Have you thought about where you want the bride and groom to first meet?"

Of course, he immediately thought about the connection he'd felt with Meg when they'd met in Liz's office. "What if we're at a party and our eyes meet across a crowded room? We could instinctively move toward one another until we're finally close enough for me to say something that makes her laugh."

Meg's cheeks flushed lightly, and he wondered if she realized that the two of them had been his inspiration for his scene idea.

"I like it. And what about the proposal?"

He turned the question back on her this time. "What would your fantasy proposal be?"

"It would take place outside." She half closed her eyes as she pictured the scene. "It would be in the moonlight, on the beach."

"Then that's what we'll do."

Meg's eyes snapped open. "Are you sure? Just because it's my idea of a perfect proposal, doesn't mean you have to use it."

"You're the expert here. In fact, what do you say we go outside right now to check out the private cove?" He handed Meg one of the cupcakes, then took the other for himself. "Let's take these for sustenance."

Meg was the picture of grace as she led them out of her office, through the building, and into the gardens. Now that the rain had finally slacked off, the flowers were opening back up to face the sun. But Lucas only had eyes for Meg as she took them down the path to the private beach, the sand still damp from the earlier downpour. Somehow, she even managed to be elegant as she ate her cupcake.

"Wow." He'd seen a lot of nice places on his tours around the world, but this private cove was truly incredible. "What a great spot."

"When I started work here, I couldn't believe spending time on the beach was going to be a regular part of my job."

"It really is beautiful," he said softly, looking at her instead of the ocean.

Meg flushed again, and Lucas loved that she reacted to him like that. So sweetly…and yet with a delicious hint of heat.

In the next beat, however, she directed them back to business. "Where exactly do you think we should set the proposal?"

He thought about it for a moment. "How about at the edge of the water, with the waves lapping at their feet."

Meg walked closer to the shoreline to feel it out. As she closed her eyes and tilted her head back to face the sun, he thought he saw a flash of longing on her face. And as the wind whipped at her hair, tearing a single strand loose from its careful confines, he couldn't stop himself from moving toward her. He reached out and brushed her hair back into place.

Her eyes flew open, and for a split second, longing seemed to turn to molten heat. Though she wasn't the kind of woman who would ever let a man kiss her within minutes of meeting, he couldn't help but want to slide his hands into her hair and press his lips to hers.

The buzzing of his phone in his pocket was the only thing that could have stopped him.

"I'm sorry," he said once he pulled it out and saw the message on the screen. "I have to go do a few interviews the label set up."

"That's all right. We've made a good start today. And this will give me some time to listen to your songs so that I'm fully up to speed by tomorrow."

Too soon, they were back in the Married in Malibu parking lot and he was getting on his Harley. "I'd like to take you to see a couple of other potential filming sites tomorrow, if that's all right."

"Are you planning to take me on *this*?" She looked at his motorcycle as though riding two-up was the craziest thing anyone had ever suggested.

"Ever been on a motorcycle?"

Again, he thought he saw a flash of longing in her eyes, before she shook her head. "I've heard they're not safe."

"I'd never convince you to do anything dangerous, Meg. Even if the press sometimes paints a different picture of me, I'm careful about the things—and the people—that matter to me."

* * *

As Meg watched him go, she could still feel the tingling on her cheek where he'd touched her.

No one in her mother's society world would have broken into her personal space like that. Instead, they would have left her with her hair in disarray, then gossiped about how she didn't look as put together as she should. And if any of the men in her mother's circle had dared to touch her, Meg doubted they would have made her heart beat as wildly as Lucas had.

She headed straight for Liz's office to give her boss the report she was likely waiting for. Carefully schooling her face so that none of her worries and concerns showed, Meg knocked on Liz's door.

"Meg, I'm glad you're here."

Liz smiled warmly at her, gesturing for her to take a seat. Liz's office was a comfortable space, so different from any of the rooms in Meg's childhood home. It had always felt to Meg like the atmosphere in her mother's house was made of sharp edges through which she had to carefully pick her way so that she didn't cut herself.

"I was just about to come find you to see if you and Lucas needed anything," Liz said.

"He had to leave for an interview," Meg told her. "But I think he's happy with everything we've come up with so far."

"I'm glad to hear that. Just let us know what you need, and we'll all pitch in to put it together. Travis will obviously need to manage security so news of the shoot doesn't leak, and I'm sure Daniel will be up for helping with some of the videography. Jenn and Kate and Nate can make the sets look like a real wedding is taking place. All based on your designs and vision, of course."

Again, Meg tried not to betray her nerves. Liz had

taken a big risk in hiring her when she didn't have a professional event-planning track record. Before coming to work at Married in Malibu, Meg had only ever organized parties and charity events for her mother. The idea of Lucas's entire video shoot resting on her abilities was a daunting one.

Despite Meg's attempts to play it cool, Liz obviously caught her hesitation. "I'm well aware that shooting a music video wasn't in the job description we agreed upon when I hired you. And I didn't exactly give you a chance to turn it down this morning, did I?" Liz looked apologetic. "If you don't feel this is a challenge you want to take on, I can call Lucas and let him know that he is going to need to look into other options."

"Please don't do that."

Yes, she felt like she'd been thrown into the deep end. At the same time, however, she now realized just how badly she wanted to live up to this opportunity. Not to prove something to her mother, or to Liz.

But to prove something to *herself.*

"Honestly, I really do think we're off to a good start."

"I'm glad to hear that, but don't forget that I'll be here if you need me to help with anything. In fact, why don't we work out what the others can do to help, which will hopefully take some of the pressure off you."

"The song is about finding true love," Meg explained, "so we will need to set up the main hall the way we do for a normal wedding, plus have an amazing cake, a gorgeous wedding dress, and guests hired from a talent agency. The same goes for the woman Lucas and his director will cast to star with him in the video."

"Hiring extras shouldn't be difficult. Finding the right woman to be his screen bride might be a little harder. Although it certainly helps that Lucas is a distractingly handsome man."

"Who did I just hear my wife describing as *distractingly handsome*?"

Although Meg had never looked at Jason Lomax as anything but a friend, there was no denying that he was quite good-looking. And from the way Liz lit up, it was obvious there was absolutely no contest between him and any other man in the world.

"You, obviously." Liz stood to give him a kiss.

"Obviously," Jason teased. "And who else?"

"Our most recent client, thanks to you." Liz turned back to Meg. "Jason is the one who recommended Married in Malibu to Lucas."

"I told him you guys would make all his worries go away. There's nothing the Married in Malibu crew can't handle. My happily married niece is living proof of that."

More determined than ever to help Lucas make the best music video his fans had ever seen, Meg nodded. "You're absolutely right, Jason. In fact, Lucas and I are going to look at other locations tomorrow, so everything is right on track."

"Does that mean I can steal Liz away for lunch with a clear conscience?"

Meg grinned. "Of course you can."

But as the couple walked out of the office with Jason's arm wrapped tightly around Liz's waist, Meg couldn't ignore the small ache in the center of her chest.

A longing to be that close to another person.

And to be loved for exactly who she was.

Chapter Three

Lucas drove his restored 1964 Mustang to Married in Malibu the next morning. As much as he enjoyed the thought of Meg riding the Harley with him, he didn't want to make the mistake of pushing her too far, too fast.

She was waiting outside when he pulled up, and with the sunlight shining on her hair, she was so stunning that he nearly stalled the car.

"Good morning." As he got out to open the passenger door for her, she asked, "No motorcycle today?"

Did he dare hope that was disappointment on her face? "Not today."

She slid onto the soft leather seat, and though he thought he detected a small sigh of pleasure, she quickly schooled her expression into one that was purely professional.

"I've got a couple of places on my list to show you," he said, "but I want your honest opinion about whether you think they will be romantic enough."

"I'm not sure you should be taking my word for the most romantic spots in the area," she replied, "when there are three happy couples working at Married in Malibu who would probably be more help to you on that front."

"Like I said yesterday, your opinion is the one I want."

Initially, he had simply been considering locations that would look good through the camera lens. Between yesterday and this morning, however, his focus had turned to the kinds of places *Meg* might find romantic.

"Okay, then I promise to do my best."

"I doubt you ever do anything but your best," he murmured.

Lucas knew what it was like to carry a heavy weight on his shoulders. He wished he could ease hers, wished he knew how to make her smile and keep her smiling.

They set off, heading toward the Getty Museum. Bel Air, which was full of mansions on sprawling estates, was only a few minutes from the museum. Though Lucas could easily afford to buy one of the large homes, he wasn't sure he would feel comfortable in the old-money neighborhood, given that his upbringing hadn't been full of much money at all, old or new.

He pulled on a dark baseball cap and sunglasses as they got out of his car. Though he'd been to the Getty only a handful of times, when he'd thought about what

Meg would like, the cultural hotspot had seemed the perfect fit.

Only, it wasn't the museum that Meg seemed excited about. "Did you see the sign for the penguin sanctuary? I think it's on the next property over." She turned to him, her eyes lighting up as she suggested, "What if you and your bride-to-be go there for your first date? Maybe you could even feed the penguins?"

"I've always been a fan of penguins," he said first. And then, "Have you been to feed them before?"

"In my family, we didn't do that kind of thing. I know the Getty quite well, though. My mother thought the museum was appropriate and educational, so she had me taken over fairly often."

"What does that mean, she *had you taken over*?"

"By my nanny." She waved her hand in the air as if to erase the whole conversation. "Since you like the penguin idea, why don't we go inside to talk to one of the staff members to find out if visitors are allowed to help feed the animals."

As they headed toward the entrance, she seemed mesmerized by the people all around them, especially the families having picnics on the grass just inside the gates and couples walking hand in hand.

He smiled at her. "People are fascinating, aren't they?"

She looked a little stunned, as though he'd caught

her doing something illicit. "They are. Especially here, where everyone seems to be having such a good time."

"Me and my friends used to take the bus from Silver Lake when we were teenagers, to see what was happening in the fancy parts of town, like Beverly Hills and Bel Air. But we always ended up having more fun here with penguins."

"Is that where you grew up, in Silver Lake?"

"We lived in a little rented apartment at the back of our block." Silver Lake was interesting, diverse, and about a thousand times less glossy than he suspected Meg's childhood home had been. "My mom still lives nearby. All of her friends are there, so she won't leave, but at least she let me buy her a house with a yard. I stop in as often as I can to see her."

"That sounds wonderful. It's nice that you have a good relationship with your mother."

She sounded a little envious, but as they'd just arrived at the entrance, he didn't get a chance to ask her more about her own upbringing. Especially given that once the security guards asked him to take off his hat and glasses and realized who he was, he ended up posing for several photographs.

"Sorry about that," he said to Meg once they were inside. "I didn't want to abandon you, but I also don't want any of my fans thinking I'm an ungrateful rocker who has forgotten where he came from."

"You don't have anything to apologize for. It's great that you have such respect for your fans." They were making their way toward one of the penguin enclosures when she added, "Where you come from is important to you, isn't it?"

"I don't want to forget about my upbringing, my roots, just because I have money now. I don't want to pretend my mom didn't have to save up every cent just to make rent. Or that my first guitar came from a pawn shop."

"It did?"

"They had it in the window, and every day on the way to my part-time job at a shoe store, I'd walk past it and hope that it would still be there. My biggest fear was that someone would buy it before I could afford the beat-up old thing." He grinned, remembering the rush of finally having his own ax. "I've replaced just about every part of it over the years so I can keep playing it."

They were standing at the penguin enclosure when she said, "I love that you still play your first guitar."

"First loves, I've found, are often the very best of all."

The way Meg was looking at him, not with stars in her eyes, but as though he'd said something that really made her think, had him wanting to kiss her again.

When the penguin feeder came out with buckets of fish, the penguins all started to go wild.

"Listen to them, they're adorable!" Her face lit up at the birds' antics. And when the trainer pointed out two penguins who were holding their flippers close and said that they had been a couple for twenty years, Meg reached for Lucas's hand. "That's amazing."

He agreed—both about the penguins' long-running relationship and how good it felt to hold her hand. "It really is."

Belatedly, she seemed to realize what she'd done and let go. "I'm so sorry about that." Her cheeks had gone pink with embarrassment. "I didn't mean to invade your space. I got so excited about the penguins, I forgot to be professional."

"It's okay. I like you in my space." He hoped it didn't sound like a pickup line, because he'd never been more serious. "And you don't have to worry about being professional with me, Meg. I want you to feel comfortable about being yourself, okay?"

He couldn't quite read her expression—confusion, mixed with longing, mixed with something that looked an awful lot like hope.

Finally, she nodded. But it was quickly back to business as she said, "We should go have a quick chat with the trainer about the possibility of filming here, and then make our way to the next location."

After the trainer confirmed that it was possible to get a special permit to film in the penguin enclosure after hours while also feeding the animals and then signed a confidentiality agreement, what seemed like half the staff at the museum came to meet Lucas and take pictures. It was a good half hour more before they finally made it out of the building.

"I should have guessed that was going to happen." Meg sounded deeply apologetic. "I've never spent time with anyone as well known as you are. Although it's more than just being famous—everyone loves your music so much, that's why they're so desperate to meet you. And I wanted to tell you, I listened to your songs last night. *All* of them." She smiled, her face lighting up. "Your songs are wonderful. You're so talented."

"That means a lot coming from you." Again, he could feel how strong their connection was. Hopefully, she would soon give him a clear sign that she felt it too. Maybe if he was lucky, their next destination would inspire her to open up to him even more. "The second place I want to take you is a nearby Japanese tea garden."

He was gratified to see her eyes light up. "I love the tea garden."

After the hustle and bustle of the penguin sanctuary, the tea garden was peaceful and serene, with a gently arching bridge over a pond, carefully cut trees, and a tea house at the center.

They took their places at one of the low tables, and

though Lucas was completely out of his element, for once it didn't matter, simply because he was with Meg.

"We talked a bit about my upbringing," he said. "Now I'm curious about yours. Where did you grow up?"

"In Bel Air." Meg looked a little embarrassed as she gestured in the direction of one of the priciest areas in Los Angeles.

That explained why Meg was so polished. And also why a nanny had *taken her over* to the Getty as a kid rather than her going with one of her parents, or on her own.

"How long have you been working at Married in Malibu?"

"Since they opened their doors. Before that, actually. We all helped get the business off the ground. Everyone at Married in Malibu is so good at what they do, it's been a pleasure to work with them all."

"It's obvious that you're a great team. What did you do before you took the job?"

Meg took a long sip of her tea, as though she was trying to find a good way to phrase her response. "I organized charity events, parties, for whatever foundations and fundraisers my mother was chairing." She grimaced slightly. "That doesn't sound too impressive, does it?"

He hated that she could ever feel that way about

herself. "From everything I've seen so far, you're *very* impressive at what you do." When it looked like she was having a hard time believing him, he told her, "I mean it, Meg. I'm not someone who gives people compliments I don't mean. I really do think you're amazing."

"That's so nice of you," she said softly. "I'm not great with compliments. Where I grew up, when someone says something nice, they either want something from you—or they're getting ready to stab you in the back the moment you drop your guard."

Lucas hadn't guessed that the life of old-money people could be so cutthroat. "What made you decide to work for Liz?"

"I wanted to do something different with my life, rather than continuing to simply follow the path my mother had laid out for me." Clearly uncomfortable with talking about herself, she asked, "What about you? How did you go from saving to buy your first guitar to becoming a rock star?"

"A lot of practice." Lucas grinned. "Seriously, I was the kid who was always practicing. Before I started playing music, I didn't really fit in. I was the poor kid who never had the right clothes and didn't go to the right school. But if I was singing something I wrote, people didn't seem to care about that anymore. And the truth is that if you want to write songs, there are few things better than having real life to draw from. A normal guy singing about normal life in a normal town—it resonates with people."

"Normal." She looked pensive. "I know this might sound weird, but I can't tell you how nice *normal* sounds."

Lucas wanted to break through the walls that Meg's upbringing had built around her and show her his world. "Talking about all of this just gave me an idea for another possible location. We'll need to intersperse some stage clips into the video," he explained, "and after the mistake I made filming in the empty stadium last week, I wasn't sure which way to go. But I've just figured it out—I need to focus on where I came from for this video. A smaller, more intimate venue with hundreds of people, as opposed to tens of thousands. A friend of mine is playing The Satellite in Silver Lake tonight. Why don't you come with me to check it out?"

"You're asking me to go to a rock concert?" She made it sound like he'd just asked her to go trekking barefoot through the jungle.

"It would be a good way for you to get a feel for how to best fit the performance angle into your overall video design. Besides," he added with a grin, "I think you might really enjoy it."

Meg bit her lip. For a moment, Lucas thought she might say no. When she finally did agree to go, relief coursed through him.

Chapter Four

Lucas dropped Meg off at Married in Malibu, promising to come back to pick her up after she finished work for the day. But instead of heading upstairs to her office, she made a beeline for Malibu T and Coffee.

All of them spent a hefty portion of their salaries on hits of caffeine from the café across the street—especially Nathan, who could always be found nursing a cup of coffee.

Meg didn't have the faintest idea how to dress for a rock concert. If it had been a classical recital, she would have known exactly what outfit to wear, when to clap, and what kind of small talk to make between movements. She could have asked her friends at Married in Malibu for advice, but she didn't want them worrying that she wasn't up to the task of going to a concert with Lucas, never mind designing his rock video. Especially Liz.

In any case, Tamara Truscott, who owned the coffee shop, was likely the best potential source of help. She was not only perfectly comfortable in her own skin, she could also chat easily with absolutely anyone—whether rocker, classical aficionado, or smooth-jazz fan.

Currently ringing up a customer, Tamara looked dressed for a sunny day on the beach with a yellow cotton shirt knotted above a floral pattern sarong. Meg could never have pulled off that casual a look, but Tamara looked amazing. It was just one more reason to ask her opinion.

"Hi, Meg, what can I get you?" Tamara asked with a smile.

"A mocha, please...and maybe some advice?"

"Sounds interesting. Take a seat and I'll bring your coffee over."

Meg sat at her favorite table, which overlooked the other customers in the café, rather than the ocean. She liked to imagine what other people's lives were like—their jobs, pets, friends...and the people who loved them.

Tamara came over with two mugs and a big cinnamon roll with two forks. Sliding Meg's drink across the table, she dropped into the free seat.

"Now, what do you need advice about?" She forked up a bite of cinnamon roll and gave a little moan of pleasure.

Meg hadn't realized how hungry she was until she smelled the sugar-coated pastry. She took a delicious bite and washed it down with a sip of her drink before saying, "What to wear to a rock concert."

Tamara sputtered, almost choking on her coffee, before composing herself. "Sorry, that almost went down the wrong pipe."

"I know." Meg sighed. "I can't imagine what he was thinking, inviting me to see his rocker friends play a show tonight." She should never have agreed.

"My reaction isn't at all about where you're going tonight," Tamara said. "I just never thought the day would come when you'd come to *me* for fashion advice. You're the best-dressed person I know. By miles."

Before Meg could respond, her phone rang with her mother's ring tone. And when her mother called, she always answered. Meg's father had passed away when she was a little girl, and for the past three decades, she and her mother were each other's only family. "I'm sorry, I need to get this."

"Margaret," her mother said as soon as Meg picked up, "I'm having a handful of people from the Bel Air Arts Foundation over for dinner tonight and I need you to present a few design choices for their end-of-year ball." Judith Ashworth never bothered with preliminaries, never thought to ask how Meg was doing, or if she had time to talk. "It's nothing too time consuming."

Meg had come to dread those words, because they rarely proved to be true. And, of course, her mother assumed that she would be there with several well-crafted designs to present.

"I have plans tonight, Mother, but perhaps there is another—"

"Cancel your plans." Her mother's voice went from cheery to brusque in an instant. "Dr. Shedmeir and Mrs. Wilton are coming. I need you *here*."

Any other time, Meg would have given in. Even now, she was tempted to bend the way she always had before. But she couldn't miss out on her night with Lucas.

Not only did her job depend on it…but a voice inside her head was also telling her that if she didn't take this step out of the confines of her life tonight, she might never do it.

"I can't cancel. It's work."

"Work, work, work." Disgust rang loud and clear in her mother's voice. "That's all you ever talk about. You can't let these people push you around."

Meg wanted to point out that her mother was the only person pushing her around. Instead, she took a gentler tack. "If you let me know what you need, I should have a couple of hours this afternoon when I can sketch something. But I'm afraid I can't come to dinner tonight."

"Well, I suppose some detailed sketches could work, at least in the short term." Her mother was clearly disgruntled as she said, "I'll email the details to you." She severed the connection without saying good-bye, just as she hadn't bothered with a hello.

Meg shot an apologetic glance at her friend. "Sorry about that."

"Don't apologize. I get how family stuff is. Now, tell me more about where you're going tonight—and who you're going with."

"It's a client." Meg leaned in closer, so no one else would hear. "It's Lucas Crosby, and I don't want to embarrass him by showing up looking like his accountant."

"Trust me, you could *never* look like his accountant. But if you're serious about fitting in…" Tamara studied her in silence for a moment. "Do you have any darker, more formfitting pants? Maybe in leather?"

"Leather?" Meg tried to imagine herself in leather pants, but she just couldn't picture it.

"Okay," Tamara said, laughing at Meg's horrified expression, "then what about dark jeans and a well-cut leather jacket?" She gestured to one of her customers who was wearing a cute brown leather jacket.

"I could wear that, I suppose." She bit her lip. "I'll definitely have to go shopping, though."

She got up, and to her surprise, Tamara got up too.

Her friend grinned. "Someone has to make sure that you don't leave the store before you find the perfect leather jacket."

"But the café—"

"Will be perfectly fine in the care of my part-time help," Tamara assured her. "Besides, when else will I have the chance to watch you getting ready for a rock concert with *Lucas Crosby*?"

Nate walked over just as Meg was sliding into the passenger seat of Tamara's car. "What's going on?"

Tamara lowered her voice, but even so, Meg caught her words. "It feels like love's in the air again. I really don't know what it is with you guys across the street, but something tells me Cupid has struck again."

Love?

Tamara was wrong. Tonight wasn't even a date. This was work.

And Meg knew the worst mistake she could possibly make would be to fall in love with her client.

Chapter Five

Lucas felt as excited as a teenager on prom night when he went to pick Meg up. Normally, it took playing to a full stadium for him feel that way. And when he saw her, looking more beautiful than any other woman ever had, he lost his breath.

The first day they'd met, she'd been stunning in high-end fashion. This morning, she'd been gorgeous in a sharply cut business suit. But seeing her in leather and denim, with her hair unbound and her lips slicked pink and glossy...

He was speechless as he got out of his car and opened the passenger door. Not only because she was beautiful, but because it was obvious that she had made an effort to fit into his world tonight. He'd never thought someone from her background would ever willingly dive into his.

"It's all wrong, isn't it?" She ran a hand through her hair, starting to twist it back into a bun. "I look like I'm trying too hard, don't I?"

"Are you kidding?" He reached for her hand and gently pulled it away from her hair, so that the locks fell free again. "You look *amazing*. You always do, no matter what you're wearing, or how you style your hair." When she finally smiled at him, shy and sweet and innately sensual all at the same time, he nearly lost his breath all over again.

Traffic was surprisingly light as they made their way to The Satellite. Lucas hadn't played the venue in years, but he'd always thought that it was the perfect size for a band to really be able to communicate with the audience.

Lucas put on a low-brimmed baseball cap and led Meg toward the door. The security staff were expecting them and let them in with a minimum of fuss. A sizable crowd had already gathered in front of the stage, where the warmup act was about to start. Though he knew he'd been spotted the moment they walked inside—the numerous phone flashes gave it away—he appreciated the rare space he and Meg were being given. As though the other audience members understood that this was an important night for them.

"There aren't any seats." Meg was clearly surprised.

"You'll want to be on your feet. Trust me."

She met his eyes. "I wouldn't have come here with you tonight if I didn't trust you."

Did she have any idea how much that meant to him?

In his business, managers stole from their clients, promoters cheated musicians out of their fair share of the concert take, and even your own band could be hammered by infighting.

Lucas wasn't used to trust being given easily, and something told him Meg didn't usually give it easily.

"Can you feel the excitement?" From the brightness in her eyes as she took everything in, he hoped she did.

"I really can. It's so different from the opera."

"I didn't see my first opera until I was in my mid-twenties," he told her, "but I've always felt the excitement there too."

"It's more muted than this, though." She looked around the club, where music was pumping from the speakers while the crowd assembled. "Like everyone is too concerned about propriety to let out what they really feel."

The words were barely out of her mouth when the lights went down and the support act ran out onto the stage. They were a local group: loud, energetic, and still obviously finding their feet. A couple of them could play extremely well, but they didn't play *together* yet.

Even so, their fans danced and cheered. Meg swayed her hips a little bit, which Lucas hoped was a good sign. Although now that the show had started, and the lights were down, he couldn't see her face well enough to know for sure if she was having a good time.

Twenty minutes later, in the break between bands, he led her over to the bar. Thankfully, with the lights down and his cap pulled low over his eyes, he continued to blend into the crowd just enough. He gave silent thanks to his fans for keeping things low-key tonight.

"What would you like to drink?"

"White wine." Meg frowned. "Unless I should be drinking beer like everyone else seems to be?"

"If you want to dance, you dance. If you want to sing, sing. And if you want to drink white wine, drink white wine. So long as you aren't hurting anyone, there aren't any rules here that you have to follow."

"I like that," she said in a voice soft enough that he read her lips more than heard what she said. *"No rules."*

He breathed a sigh of relief. Maybe he hadn't blown it, after all, by bringing her here.

When they moved back into the crowd, he took her to the place that he considered the sweet spot—it combined a great view of the stage with the optimal audible experience.

As soon as his friend's band took the stage and started to play, it was clear that they were ready for the big time. They'd polished their sound, had attracted a rabid fan base, and fit together like a well-oiled machine, supporting each other so that each musician in the group shone even brighter as part of the whole.

What's more, they connected brilliantly with their

audience. Which, Lucas was pleased to realize midway through the first song, included Meg. She wasn't screaming or jumping up and down like the others, but she had a big smile on her face as her body moved to the music.

He loved watching her let herself go—the way she listened with rapt intensity, while taking in the light show and the thrill of the crowd.

An hour and a half later, after two encores that had everyone happily hoarse from singing along and cheering, the show came to an end. Lucas was surprised to realize that he'd been so busy watching Meg enjoy herself that he hadn't analyzed the music and performance the way he normally would. Instead, he'd simply enjoyed himself. More than he had in a very long time.

After the last echoes faded away, Meg turned to him with a smile. "I loved it." She seemed to catch herself, adding, "Not that I thought I wouldn't. It's just, not having been to a show like this before—" She blew out a breath. "I'm normally good at not saying the wrong thing or being inappropriate. But with you, my unfiltered thoughts keep spilling out."

"I'm glad that you feel you can say what you're thinking, and what you're feeling, when you're with me. In my world, people tend to tell me what they think I want to hear. You're not being inappropriate—you're being honest. And as far as I'm concerned, that's a really great thing."

* * *

Meg felt as though she were floating as they made their way backstage.

Why had she waited her whole life to go to a rock concert? Okay, so the music had been incredibly loud. And she wasn't sure that she would want to run into some of the audience members alone in a dark alley. But she had absolutely loved the feeling, technique, and passion in the music—just as much as she had loved being part of the dancing, overjoyed crowd.

Best of all, though, had been Lucas standing beside her. He was so warm and solid and strong that she knew he'd never let anything bad happen to her. And then, when he'd said all those lovely things about how much he loved her honesty…

Truly, her heart was so full she thought it might burst.

Backstage, large men in faded black T-shirts with the word STAFF on the back were carefully packing away cables, microphones, instruments, and stands. She knew how much went into putting on an elaborate, high-budget wedding. But she could only imagine the behind-the-scenes planning that went into putting on a concert, whether in a venue like this or a stadium like the ones Lucas played in.

A half-dozen people on the stage crew called out Lucas's name. As he introduced her to each person, she was amazed that he not only knew their names, he also knew all about their kids and grandkids. Even their dogs!

A short while later, he brought her into a dressing room where the four members of the band were drinking beer, looking like they'd just run a marathon. After the incredibly energetic show they'd put on, she understood why.

At first glance, they looked like members of a biker gang, with extravagant beards, leather pants, long hair, tattoos, and piercings. But from the grins on their faces when they spotted Lucas, she could tell immediately that they were all really nice guys.

"Lucas!" The lead singer pushed up from his seat. "I thought I spotted you in the crowd."

"I wasn't going to miss it. And I wanted to bring my friend to see you play." She was touched that he already considered her a friend. "Meg, this is Brian, Saul, Ken, and Jon. Guys, this is Meg."

The band made room for her on the couch, and someone got her a glass of wine. "What did you think of the show?" Brian asked.

"It was amazing. There was so much *energy*." Even now, she could feel the music pulsing through her. "I'm so glad Lucas brought me."

"We're working on a video together," he explained. Clearly, he trusted these guys not to leak the details of his top-secret shoot. "Tonight was part of our research."

"Are you a producer?" Saul asked Meg.

"Actually, I work at Married in Malibu. I usually design weddings instead of music videos."

Ken's eyebrows went up. "I've read about that place in celebrity magazines. It sounds pretty ritzy."

"Since when do you read celebrity magazines?" Lucas asked Ken, laughing.

"Since when do you *read*?" Jon joked, as the men fell into good-natured teasing.

In the world in which Meg had grown up, everyone acted polite on the surface, but could turn cruel at the drop of a hat. Whereas here, it was clear that these men would be there for each other when it really mattered, no matter what.

"We're heading on to a party," Brian told them. "Why don't the two of you join us?"

Meg was torn. She was tempted to say yes. But she was already so full of sensation, so much sound and color. What she really wanted to do was go home and let it all soak in.

Lucas seemed to sense that, because he shook his head. "We'll take a rain check this time, guys. Great show."

On the way out to Lucas's car, several fans stopped him to ask for autographs and photos. But she didn't mind in the least. His music made their lives better—and they wanted him to know how happy he made them.

Once they hit the road and she realized he was taking her back to Married in Malibu, instead of to her house, she asked, "Would you mind dropping me back at my place? My car's fine where it is for the night."

She rarely invited visitors to her house. A tenth the size of her mother's, Meg's home was her sanctuary. But now that Lucas had shown her part of his world tonight, she found she wanted to show him a little bit of hers, even if he only stayed long enough to see her front garden.

"Your friends were really nice," she said with a smile.

"So are yours over at Married in Malibu. They seem like a great crew."

"I'm lucky to have met them all."

She couldn't imagine what her life would be like without them. On second thought, she could imagine it all too clearly. Without her friends at Married in Malibu, she knew her life would be nothing more than the usual grind of galas and charity events, using her talents in whatever limited way her mother told her to.

"Actually, I think your friends are lucky to have met *you*," Lucas said, turning to meet her gaze. "I know I feel lucky."

She was blushing profusely as he pulled up in front of her home. As he walked her to her front door, she noticed nearly all the lights were off in her neighbors' homes.

"I didn't realize how late it is." She was still buzzing after the concert, wide awake even though she would normally have been asleep by now. "Is this what people always feel after seeing a great show?"

"If you mean feeling invincible, like I could do anything, like I don't ever want this moment to end?" He held her gaze. "Yes, that's exactly how I feel tonight."

With his gorgeous face lit by the nearly full moon above them, Meg couldn't lie to herself any longer. It wasn't just the great concert that made her feel like she could dance all night long.

It was Lucas.

"I had a really great time with you, Meg." His voice was deep and warm. "Thank you for coming with me. I wouldn't have enjoyed the show nearly as much without you."

She was on the verge of telling him that tonight had been, hands down, the best night of her life. But before she could, he leaned in, and for a moment—just a moment—she dared to dream that she might feel his lips pressing against hers.

Of course, she knew she needed to be cautious and that she couldn't make the mistake of falling in love with him when she was simply supposed to be his video designer. But the truth was that if Lucas kissed her now, she didn't think she would have enough self-control to push him away…or to keep from relishing every second of his kiss.

In the end, his lips only brushed her cheek.

Even that was enough to stay with her, long after he'd said good night and driven away.

Chapter Six

With her car still at Married in Malibu, Meg thought about taking an Uber to work the next morning. But Lucas had said he and his friends used to take the bus to explore different areas when they were teenagers. She wasn't sure how she'd gone this many years without taking a bus, but she was determined to rectify that situation immediately.

Not only did the bus turn out to be great for people-watching, but the route traversed some interesting-looking areas that she'd never been in before. One day soon, she would go back and spend more time exploring.

A text came in from her mother when Meg was still a few miles out from work.

Everyone liked the ideas I presented last night. Call me so that we can discuss the detailed plan for when you run the event. I need you to have everything ready for dinner the day after tomorrow.

As usual, her mother had assumed Meg was free for

dinner, regardless of the night of the week. What's more, she'd also assumed that her daughter would happily set up and run the charity event. And why wouldn't she, when Meg had always done exactly that?

Today, however, instead of getting right back to her mother, Meg made a mental note to call her later as she pulled out her notebook to jot down an idea the local scenery had just given her for one of Lucas's film sets. For the rest of the ride, the message on her phone was forgotten as she continued to sketch ideas, wanting to capture the excitement of last night's show before she lost hold of the feeling. The only problem was, once she put some thoughts down on paper, they didn't look quite right. She felt as though she was circling the right ideas, but not quite getting to the heart of them.

When Meg arrived at Married in Malibu, Kate was trimming back roses while chatting with Jenn, who must be taking a break from the kitchen for a few minutes. Her friends clearly took great joy in their jobs, despite the seemingly endless work of nurturing the large garden throughout each season—and coming up with brilliant new cake flavors and designs—for every wedding.

Meg walked over to say hello. "Good morning."

"You look bright-eyed and bushy-tailed this morning," Jenn noted. "I hope that means everything is going well with Lucas's video?"

Meg tried to fight back a blush, but it was difficult when she couldn't stop thinking about the feel of his lips on her cheek last night—and the way he'd said, *I wouldn't have enjoyed the show nearly as much without you.*

"It's going great, thanks. Although—" Normally, she wouldn't have dared admit to anything less than perfect control over every detail. Yet she could tell Jenn and Kate the truth, couldn't she? After all, they were her friends. "I'm having a little trouble translating my ideas into concrete designs."

"I totally get that," Kate said. "Sometimes when I'm putting displays together, it takes *hours* staring at the plants before I finally get it right."

"It's the same for me in the kitchen," Jenn agreed. "Sometimes it's not until I've baked a cake a dozen times that I finally get the look and taste just right."

Kate reached out to touch Meg's arm. "I wish the rest of us could do more to take the pressure off you. Maybe if the three of us take a few minutes to go through the details for the wedding as a team, that might help crystallize your ideas for the video as a whole?"

Meg hesitated for a moment. She was used to working alone. But then, she'd never had friends who were not only experts in their fields—but who would also never think of shooting down her ideas in order to prop up their own.

Yet again, it struck her how different working at Married in Malibu was from helping out with her mother's many causes. At the upper echelons of society, everything was about status, about proving why you deserved the most praise, the most accolades. Whereas here, Meg's friends genuinely cared about seeing her succeed.

"It needs to be a rock 'n' roll wedding," Meg said, "but I don't know exactly how to get that across, apart from using a few big, bold colors." She thought about the colors Lucas seemed to favor. "Blues. Different shades of charcoal, with an occasional hint of purple."

"I can make a contemporary, angular, multitiered cake for maximum impact," Jenn offered.

"And I can combine striking blue and purple flowers to echo the theme of Jenn's cake."

"A classic white dress would really stand out as a contrast, wouldn't it?" When both women nodded, Meg said, "I really like everything you've both suggested. Of course, I'll have to run all of this by Lucas."

"I haven't seen a client yet who's gone against your recommendations," Kate noted. "They know when they're in the hands of an expert."

"Speaking of expert hands," Jenn said, "what's Lucas Crosby *really* like?"

Kate teasingly elbowed Jenn in the ribs. "Does Daniel know you have a crush?"

"It's not a crush," their star baker said, though her cheeks had gone slightly pink. "I've just been a fan for a while and can't help but wonder if he's as great as he seems."

Meg had never sat with a group of girlfriends and talked about a guy before. Honestly, she wasn't even sure she knew where to start. "He *is* great," she finally said.

"You've got to give us more than that!" Jenn urged.

"Well...he took me to a rock concert last night. It was amazing."

"Sounds like Jenn isn't the only one with a crush," Kate murmured.

Meg shook her head. "I... He..."

"I shouldn't be teasing you," Kate said. "It's just that he's *so* famous and *so* good-looking."

"Kate's right. You know how much I love Daniel, but even I was a little bit nervous meeting Lucas two days ago."

Had it been only two days? Meg could hardly imagine a time when Lucas hadn't been in her life.

"I was really nervous at first," she admitted. "And awkward. But he's so nice. And kind. And open and honest too."

Kate didn't look at all surprised. "The famous people coming to get married here are still ordinary underneath, aren't they?"

But Meg had a hard time thinking of Lucas as *ordinary*.

How could she, when he was extraordinary in every

sense that mattered?

"Just remember," Kate added, "if you need our help again, we're here for you."

"Thanks, but—"

"But nothing," Jenn said. "You're one of us. Part of our posse."

"Don't forget that all of us want to help you however we can," Kate added. "You're not in this alone, Meg."

Meg's heart had felt fit to burst from the excitement of last night. Already this morning, it was overflowing again.

All her life, she'd felt like she was balancing on a high wire with no one waiting to catch her if she fell. Now, she had a group of friends who would not only catch her—they would make sure she didn't have to get up on the high wire in the first place.

Impulsively, she reached out to hug both women. And when they hugged her back, it was one of the nicest feelings in the world.

* * *

Lucas found Meg sitting beneath an oak tree, sketching in a notebook. She looked up with a smile when he called her name.

"I'm so glad you're here. I've had so many ideas since last night!" She handed him the notebook. "Here's how I'm thinking we could set up the wedding scene."

Her sketch combined rock 'n' roll with classic elegance, and Lucas knew in his gut that it would be perfect.

"As I hope you can see from what I've drawn, I'd like to give the hall the feel of a chapel. That way, when we shoot you waiting for your bride—"

"I wouldn't wait for her at the altar," Lucas interrupted. "I wouldn't be able to keep from breaking away from my best man to meet her halfway up the aisle."

Meg smiled. "You're right. And I think you'd reach for her hands, knowing this was the moment you'd been waiting for your whole life."

Lucas instinctively wrapped his hand around hers. He could feel the softness of her skin, so different from the calluses that years of playing guitar had given him. This close, he could also smell the sweet scent of her perfume.

"I'd walk beside her to the altar," he said softly.

"And then we could show you saying your vows while your song is playing," Meg said. "I know your lyrics to 'Perfect Moments' are everything I would want someone to say to me on my wedding day."

It always meant a great deal to him to know that one of his songs moved someone enough for them to play it during a special occasion, or that his lyrics had helped them to get through a hard time in their life. Yet, Meg saying that his lyrics would be her idea of perfect wedding vows made him speechless.

"And then after you exchange rings," she continued, "you'll walk out of the church together—"

"Wait. You've missed something." With their hands still linked, he couldn't stop himself from drawing her closer. "We need to show the first kiss as husband and wife."

"You're right." She was flushing lightly. "And when you kiss each other, everything else around you should fade away."

"That's perfect, Meg. Although, there's still something we need to figure out—what kind of kiss should it be?"

"What do you mean, what *kind* of kiss?" Her cheeks had flushed a deeper rose by now, but she hadn't let go of his hands.

"Should it be soft and gentle? Should I brush my fingers over her cheek and take the time to drink in her scent before my lips feather against hers?"

As Lucas spoke, instead of some actress that they still needed to cast, it was Meg's lips he imagined tasting, Meg's hair he wanted to run his fingers through.

"Should I take my time exploring that first kiss, because I know I'll have the rest of my life to share with her? Or should all the moments we've spent together have built up until I can't hold back any longer from giving her a passionate *forever* kiss?"

Chapter Seven

All Lucas had done was describe the kiss, but Meg could practically taste his lips against hers. And when he switched to the possibility of the more passionate kiss, it was all she could do to keep from gasping in anticipation of it.

She wanted to kiss him so much it hurt—just like every other groupie who had ever thrown herself at him.

Thankfully, his phone rang before she could make that critical mistake.

"Sorry," he said as he drew his hands from hers to answer the call. "That's the ring tone for my sound engineer. I have to get this in case there's a problem with mastering the final track." After a short conversation, he put the phone back into his pocket. "Just like I thought, there's a problem at the recording studio that I've got to sort out."

"Nothing serious, I hope?"

"It's nothing unexpected at this stage in the game. I just hate having to leave when our ideas are falling into place."

"Actually, now that we've figured out the basics for the wedding, I can start getting everything ready while you're gone. Would that be okay with you?"

"Whatever you do, Meg, you have my complete trust. I'll be back as soon as I can."

For a moment, she thought he might give her another kiss on the cheek, just as he had the night before. In the end, however, he headed off to his car with only a wave.

She should have gone inside immediately to put their ideas into practice. But her mind was still cluttered with echoes of the sweet, then passionate, kisses he had described.

Kisses she'd be dreaming of from now on…

"Penny for your thoughts?" Liz asked when she found Meg standing in the middle of the rose garden.

"I like Lucas." Meg couldn't believe she'd just said that out loud. Especially to her *boss*. She half expected the earth to crack open and swallow her up. Either that or she'd be fired on the spot.

"I can see why," Liz replied. "He seems like a really nice guy."

"No, I mean I *like* him."

Liz grinned. "I knew what you meant the first time."

"But I'm not supposed to fall for him!"

Liz cocked her head. "Why not?"

"He's a client."

Instead of agreeing, her boss shrugged. "He's not here to marry someone. And he's not seeing anyone, is he?"

"I don't think so. But he has women falling for him left, right, and center. Trust me, I've seen the way people react to him everywhere we go. He doesn't need me falling for him too, especially when I'm supposed to be focusing my energy on his video."

"First of all, it sounds like you're doing fantastic work for his video so far. And second, what makes you think he's not falling for you right back?"

"You can't be serious. He's a rock star. And I'm..." Meg held out her arms, gesturing to herself. "Well, I'm just me."

"Have you ever looked in a mirror?" Liz asked. "You're not only beautiful, you're sweet, and you're smart too. Any man would be lucky to have you, rock star or not."

Meg couldn't quite take in what Liz was saying, though, not when all she wanted was out of this minefield of a conversation. "The only thing I know for sure is that I've got to nail Lucas's video."

"I have every confidence in you," Liz told her. "In fact, the reason I came outside to find you is to let you know that I've spoken with Anne in the San Francisco office. She's agreed to put aside her other commissions and create a wedding gown for the video. As soon as we can, we need to let her know who will be wearing it so that we can send over the measurements. Is the casting call still on for tomorrow?"

"Yes, the casting is still on track." Meg smiled at her boss, even though her stomach was sinking at the thought of hiring someone to stand at the altar with Lucas, to hold his hands, to stare deep into his eyes—and worst of all, to kiss him.

While Meg stood on the sidelines, wishing it could be her instead.

⋆ ⋆ ⋆

Jason Lomax was waiting for Lucas in a corner booth at the brewpub where they had agreed to meet for a drink. On his way to the table, Lucas signed four autographs and posed for six selfies. He was always up for chatting with his fans, but though they might love what he did, and felt a connection to his music, it wasn't the same thing as genuinely knowing one another. It was why getting together with a true friend like Jason was so important.

With Jason, Lucas was just one of the guys—not a rock star or a sex symbol. It was exactly how Meg treated him too—like a normal person.

"Hanging out with you reminds me of why I like being a reclusive author so much," Jason noted when

Lucas finally slid into the booth.

"Between your niece and the countless number one bestselling books you've written, you're plenty famous. I'm sure most of the people in here have read your books. They just don't happen to know what you look like."

"If that's your way of saying I'm the one who should buy the first round, I'm two steps ahead of you." As if on cue, a waitress dropped off two glasses of Guinness. "So, how's everything going with the video?"

"Meg is exactly the person I've been looking for." He smiled as he thought about her. "We've been scouting locations all over SoCal for the video."

"So spending time with her is just about the video, huh?" Jason shot him a knowing look, obviously having caught Lucas's goofy smile. "Meg's a great person. You could do a lot worse."

Clearly, Jason was biased because he was in love with Liz. Still, as far as Lucas was concerned, there was no one smarter, no one kinder, no one lovelier than Meg. "She's incredible."

"Man," Jason said with a laugh, "you've got it bad."

"Who wouldn't? Meg's intelligent, beautiful, creative—and she's also way too good for a guy like me."

"You're kidding, right? You're one of the biggest rock stars in the world. I very much doubt that Meg would kick you out of her bed for eating crackers."

But what Lucas felt for Meg had nothing to do with his fame or fortune. She wasn't the kind of woman who was going to fall into his arms simply because he was a rock star. Heck, she'd barely even heard of him until he came to Married in Malibu to shoot his video.

"I really don't think I'm the kind of guy she ever thought she could spend her life with. The two of us are from such different backgrounds. She grew up with *servants*. Can you imagine a guy like me trying to fit into that world?"

"If you want it badly enough, then yes, I can imagine it. The question is whether *you* can."

"It's not just about me," Lucas continued. "How would her bastion-of-society mother react to some leather-clad guitar player dating her daughter?"

"She'd probably go ballistic." Jason had the nerve to grin as he added, "But then, that's kind of the point of mothers-in-law. Seriously, though, Meg's more than capable of making up her own mind—and sticking to it. After all these months, I know her pretty well. She might be from a high-society world, but she's not a hothouse flower about to wilt at any moment. Do you think Liz would have hired her if she wasn't strong and brilliant?" Jason put down his beer, clearly ready to drive his point home. "All I can tell you is that when I looked at Liz the first time, I knew. She was the only one who mattered. The only woman I would ever love."

There was no question that love had made Jason a better man. Heck, these days some of the stories he wrote even had happy endings. Still, Lucas was compelled to point out, "Didn't it take you ten years to end up together?"

"It did. And I'd hate to see you and Meg make the same mistake."

Chapter Eight

The next day, the auditions for the female lead in Lucas's music video quickly went from bad to worse. Seb, the director, had taken to yelling more and more loudly as the auditions wore on. "No, no, no! That's not right. More passion! From the top!"

Meg had taken on the role of greeting each new applicant and showing her where to wait for her audition. There were redheads, blondes, brunettes—and each was more stunning than the next, sauntering into the building in their street clothes with such flair it looked like they were wearing designer outfits instead.

"Walk toward Lucas looking like you're about to say *I do*," Seb ordered the current candidate, "not like you're some nervous fangirl! And Lucas, try to remember that she's your one and only."

Although the director was a bit intense, Meg had to admit he had a point. A surprising number of the actresses were reacting to Lucas like gushing fans. One even asked if she could take a selfie with him. And among the ones who could act, none of them was conveying nearly enough of a connection with him. Lucas was also more wooden than she'd ever seen him.

Unfortunately, even though they auditioned another dozen actresses, trying the scene in different ways, with different approaches—none of it made a difference.

"It's not working," Lucas said, obviously frustrated.

"I have an idea," Meg said before she could stop herself.

Seb peered at her. "Who the heck are you?"

"Meg is in charge of design," Lucas told him in the hardest voice she'd ever heard him use, as though he thought his director had just insulted her. "I introduced you this morning." His voice was far more mild as he turned back to her and asked, "What do you have in mind?"

"No, I don't want to *hear* your idea, I want to *see* it," Seb insisted. "Lucas, go stand by the altar. And you..."

"Meg." She almost laughed at how difficult he found remembering her name. Lucas, on the other hand, didn't seem to find it funny at all.

"Okay, Meg, start by the door like we've done with the others—and blow me away with your idea."

Meg's breathing sped up along with her heart rate as she got into place and waited for her cue. She hoped she wouldn't mess this up too badly.

"Action!" Seb called.

When Meg stepped forward, she felt as nervous as if this really were her wedding—especially when she saw Lucas standing at the altar, looking at her as though she was the only woman who had ever, and would ever, matter to him.

The next thing she knew, Lucas had broken away from the altar. Just as they had the first time they met, her feet took her toward him. Soon, she found herself in his arms, staring into his eyes, dreaming of his kiss now more than ever. Next thing she knew, he'd tucked her arm through his and they were making their way up the aisle.

"Yes, that's it!" Seb sounded happy for the first time all day. "Meg, the part is yours."

"Excuse me?" Meg looked at Seb, certain she must have heard him wrong.

If she had, though, why would Lucas be saying, "Please do it, Meg. Please be my bride."

"But I'm not an actress."

"Want to bet?" Seb motioned them over. "Look at the magic I just caught on camera and I guarantee you won't be able to tell me that again."

Meg barely kept herself from covering her eyes with her hands as Seb played the scene back for them. She hadn't thought he'd actually *film* her idea…

"Look at the chemistry between you."

"But I didn't mean for—" Meg began. She didn't get

a chance to finish.

"And those cheekbones!" Seb was clearly in raptures. "You were made for the screen. Why have we wasted all day with these pathetic auditions when we could have hired you at the start and got on with filming?"

Meg shook her head, which felt like it was whirling. "I never expected any of this. I'm not even sure if I can do it."

"Well, you'd better get sure quickly, because we start filming tomorrow morning." With that, Seb made one heck of a stage exit, not giving Meg another chance to argue.

"I know I'm putting even more pressure on you now by asking you to be my bride," Lucas said, "but will you at least think about it? You have to admit we have amazing chemistry together on screen."

On screen, off screen, *everywhere*, as far as Meg was concerned. But being in his video was a big leap. The biggest leap she'd ever taken in her life.

The simple act of coming to work at Married in Malibu had been going against her mother's wishes. But her job had all been behind the scenes so far, out of the public eye. Even the work she'd done with Lucas had been background work, planning scenes where he'd be the focus of attention, not her. Not one single person who had wanted a picture of Lucas had pointed a camera at her, even at the concert where she'd practically been his date.

But if she co-starred in his video, there was no way she would be able to keep her mother or her mother's social circle out of the loop.

If it were anyone other than Lucas asking her to do this, she wouldn't think twice about saying no. But truthfully, the thought of anyone other than herself walking down the aisle with him during filming was almost too much to bear.

"I'll think about it," she finally managed.

* * *

Meg was so twisted up over Lucas's offer to star with him that she nearly skipped girls' night at Jenn and Daniel's house. But not only did she know that she could be her less-than-perfect self with these women—she also knew it would help to discuss things with them.

Daniel and the kids were out at a movie, but had made plenty of cupcakes and cookies before they left. Meg, Liz, and Amy had brought wine, Kate had made an elderflower cordial for everyone, and Tamara had brought a coffee liqueur.

"Liz, you start our round-table catch-up," Tamara said as soon as everyone had a drink. "How are things going?"

"Everything is perfect," Liz said with a happy smile.

"You've got to give us more than that," Tamara

urged.

"Well, the business is going great. I get to spend my free time with the man I love. And I have the best group of friends." They all toasted to that.

Liz turned to Amy, who was making a sketch of the group with a lime green and a royal blue crayon that Jenn's kids had left out. "What about you, Amy? Is everything working out as well as it seems to be?"

"And if you say that things are *perfect*," Tamara teased, "there will be trouble."

"But things really are perfect." Amy managed to catch the chocolate chip cookie Tamara threw her way before it hit her on the nose. "Everything with Travis feels so right—exactly how I dreamed it would be when we first met all those years ago. I'm absolutely loving painting wedding portraits. *And* I still can't believe my paintings are going to be hanging in a gallery soon."

They all toasted again, and then Amy said, "Okay, Jenn, you're next in line to tell us how perfect your life is." When Tamara groaned at the word *perfect* they all laughed.

"Honestly, life with Daniel and our kids is pretty darn close to that."

Meg thought it was great how Jenn said *our* kids, rather than *his* kids. The four of them fit so naturally together as a family that there didn't appear to be any seams anymore.

"I'm happy for all of you," Tamara said. "I really am. But for those of us who have been single for what feels like forever, it can be an awful lot of *true love* to swallow. Which is why my big news is that I've decided to look into the full 'bean-to-cup' route for my café with a farmer I've connected with in Brazil."

The five of them waited for her to say something about Nate. But she seemed utterly oblivious to the sparks that shot off whenever Married in Malibu's computer specialist dropped by her coffee shop. Which, some days, was practically hourly.

Tamara turned to Kate. "Your turn."

"I'm toying with cross-breeding some really gorgeous begonias." Kate grinned. "Which, before you ask, are far better than men, as far as I'm concerned. They smell good, they look great, and they never give me grief if I want to spend more time in the garden than washing my hair to look pretty for a date."

Everyone laughed, then inevitably shifted their gazes to Meg.

"Any news about the gorgeous rock star you've been spending all your time with?" Tamara asked.

Meg bit her lip. Thus far, Liz was the only one who knew that Meg had a bit of a crush on Lucas. But that wasn't even the biggest news.

"I would have brought this up with you before, Liz, but it all happened so quickly at the end of the auditions that I didn't have a chance." She took a breath, then said, "None of the actresses were working out, and after I ended up walking through the scene with Lucas…well…he asked if *I* would do it."

Several gasps sounded in the room, with Tamara enthusing, "You guys are going to look *so* good together on camera."

"I agree," Jenn said with a nod. "Right from the start, when you met in Liz's office, it was obvious that you two have great chemistry."

Amy and Kate were both nodding, as well. "I can completely see why he picked you."

Only Liz hung back. "Are *you* okay with doing this, Meg? I know this job feels like a train barreling down the tracks, but I meant it when I said I would step in if you need me to."

"Well, I haven't actually agreed to do it yet. Mostly because the thought of being in a music video seems crazy."

"I understand why you feel that way," Liz said, "but the truth is that sometimes crazy works. There are plenty of people who would say that it was crazy for Rose and RJ to open up a wedding venue for celebrities. And there are plenty more who would think it was crazy for me to get back together with Jason after ten years apart."

"Sometimes you just have to take a risk and see what

happens," Jenn agreed. "And sometimes it turns out better than you could have imagined. Several of us in this room are proof of that."

"What's the worst that could happen?" Amy asked.

"My mother freaks out, disinherits me, and never speaks to me again," Meg said automatically.

Meg could tell by the weight of Tamara's stare that her friend was about to hit her with a doozy of a question.

"Are you living your life or your mother's?"

Meg knew the answer in her heart, even if she couldn't have voiced it out loud before. Not until her friends had proved that they'd support her through thick and thin.

"My life."

"No matter what any of us say," Liz reminded her, "the only thing that matters is what you feel comfortable with. If you say no, the answer is no. And if you say yes—then we will all do whatever we can to support your starring turn in Lucas Crosby's video."

Meg looked into her friends' faces. Fun, intelligent, warm women who would never steer her in the wrong direction.

Especially when it was the path her heart had already taken.

"Yes. I'll do it." Her heart was pounding hard in her chest, but she was pleased and surprised to realize that it was more from anticipation than from fear.

"You should text him right now," Kate urged. "I'm sure he's not only waiting to hear from you, but also, if they really are planning on beginning to shoot the video tomorrow, I suspect the director and crew are on pins and needles wondering if the 'bride' has signed on yet."

Meg took out her phone and nervously typed: *I'll do it.*

His answer took less than five seconds to come back, as though he really had been waiting for her decision: *You've made my night. I'll give Seb the good news. See you tomorrow when we start filming.*

"This is *amazing*," Jenn said as she refilled their glasses for another toast.

"You're going to star in a video with Lucas Crosby!" Tamara practically shouted the words, she was so overjoyed.

They were all raising their glasses for a toast, when the full breadth of what she'd agreed to finally hit Meg.

"Oh my God, now that I'm the bride…that means I have to kiss him!" They wouldn't be filming that scene until the day after tomorrow, which meant the butterflies in her stomach would multiply a million times over by then.

"Lucky you," Tamara murmured.

Kate put a hand on Meg's shoulder. "Remember what you said to me in the garden—Lucas is a really nice guy. You're going to be fine."

"Or maybe," Amy said with a slow smile, "it will turn out much, much better than fine. Maybe it will even end up being *perfect*."

Chapter Nine

The next morning, when Meg arrived at the house they were using to film the party scene where Lucas and Meg would meet for the first time in the video, dozens of cars were already parked outside, completely taking over the street. Travis stood at the front door, carefully vetting each person who tried to enter. When he saw her, he grinned. "I'm very happy to hear you're going to star in the video, Meg. Go on in, they're expecting you."

Dozens of extras turned to check her out as she walked inside. Not only were all of them extremely attractive, they were also clearly old hands at working on sets like this.

What am I doing here? Meg asked herself.

There were so many women here who were surely more deserving of the lead role. Only the sight of Lucas waving to her from across the room kept her from turning and running out.

Slowly, she made her way over to him, past everyone who was still staring at her and the extensive lighting, makeup, styling, and film staff Seb had brought.

"I really am glad you've agreed to do this with me, Meg." Lucas's smile heated her up all over. "I promise you won't regret it."

"I just hope *you* don't regret it."

"I won't." He looked utterly certain.

She gestured toward the racks of clothes. "What do you want me to wear?"

He didn't even bother to scan her outfit. He simply looked into her eyes and said, "I like you just the way you are."

Though she knew he must be talking about her outfit of dark jeans, sleeveless silk top and ankle boots, it felt as though he was saying so much more.

"Okay…but if I turn out to be really bad at this, promise you'll tell me. You won't hurt my feelings if you decide not to use me."

"I promise," he agreed. "But I already know that you and I are perfect together."

Again, it almost seemed as though he was talking about more than just the video they were about to film. But that was surely just down to the romantic fantasies she hadn't quite been able to control where Lucas was concerned…

Hair and makeup gave her a quick once-over and then the next thing she knew, they were ready to go. For the extras, that meant dancing along with Lucas's new single. For Meg, however, it meant walking into the room, looking into his eyes, then moving close to him so that he could whisper in her ear and make her laugh.

Amazingly, each time Seb had them film the scene, Lucas *did* manage to make her laugh.

"Did I ever tell you about the time the crew put a battery-powered frog in my amplifier?"

"Put your right foot in, take your right foot out, put your right foot in and shake it all about..."

"A rock star and a wedding designer walk into a bar..."

But he didn't only make her laugh. His touch also made thrill bumps run up her arms and butterflies take flight in her stomach.

Could everyone in the room see what she was feeling?

As if to answer her silent question, Seb called out, "I can't believe how much chemistry there is between you two." The director stepped between them. "That's a wrap, so we can head over to our next set now. I've already sent a second crew over, so we should be ready to film as soon as we get there."

A half hour later, they were at the penguin sanctuary where they had started to bond for the first time, even if they'd occasionally been interrupted by Lucas's fans. Now, however, their every move would be documented by cameras as they had their first "date."

A part of her couldn't help wishing that this was a

real date. And as shooting wore on, she found herself forgetting more and more that she wasn't supposed to actually fall in love with him.

"Are you sure you haven't acted before?" Seb asked her between takes. "When you're with Lucas, I could almost believe that you really *are* in love with him." The director grinned at Lucas. "And that you're in love with her too."

Meg tried to laugh it off. "I took a few drama classes in high school," she said, hoping that it would be enough to satisfy the director.

"Well, it certainly seems to have worked. Now, on to the penguin feeding."

Soon, Meg was armed with a bucket of fish, while surrounded by very cute, but very insistent, birds. Lucas nearly fell over laughing at their attempts to grab the food from her even before she could hand it out.

The beautiful sound of his laughter had her losing another piece of her heart to him.

"I never thought I'd ever do something like this," Meg said ninety minutes later, once they were done filming with the penguins. Meg had worn thick rubber gloves and a large green jumpsuit over her clothes to keep them clean. But she hadn't minded getting a little dirty. Not when the penguins were so much fun to feed.

"You enjoyed that, didn't you?" Lucas was grinning at her as they both kicked off their guano boots, peeled off their smelly rubber gloves, and stripped out of their coveralls.

"I really did." She wrinkled her nose. "Although I'm pretty sure I'm going to need to soap up in the shower for quite a while. I don't want to smell like penguin food while we're shooting the concert scene in an hour." Fortunately, they had already been told that they could use the staff facilities to shower and clean up.

Lucas's eyes grew dark, as though he was imagining her in the shower. A shiver of desire ran through her. Though it was difficult, she forced herself to push her ridiculous imaginings away.

"I'll hop in a shower too," he said, his voice deep and sexy. "I wouldn't want to give you a reason not to stand close to me."

Didn't he realize that it would take *far* more than that to keep her from wanting to stand close to him? Really, really close...

A short while later, they left the sanctuary and crawled through traffic to get to The Satellite. She hadn't thought to bring her leather jacket, but fortunately there was one on the wardrobe rack.

The first time she'd worn leather, she'd felt like a fraud. This time, it felt exactly right. Especially when she caught the heat in Lucas's eyes whenever he looked at her.

Seb's plan was to cut between Lucas playing his new

song with his band on stage and Meg dancing and singing along to it.

She was worried that she wouldn't be able to feel the music as deeply as she should while surrounded by a bunch of cameras and strangers. But once Lucas started to sing…

Her heart was forever lost.

She'd been blown away when he'd played the acoustic guitar in her office, but watching him perform on stage was even more amazing. Especially because—despite the extras, the lights, the cameras—she felt as though he was singing the beautiful song just for her.

When the song ended, the extras cheered as though they were at a real gig, instead of a video shoot. And when Seb insisted on shooting the same scene a dozen more times, Meg was glad.

Because she never wanted today to end.

Everything she had done so far was completely outside of her comfort zone. Amazingly, it was also the most fun she'd ever had.

All because of Lucas.

* * *

Few things were more breathtaking than moonlight in Malibu. Especially when it was shining down on the most beautiful woman Lucas had ever known.

All day long, they had been surrounded by extras.

Now, as they prepared to shoot the final scene of the day—their engagement scene on the beach in Married in Malibu's private cove—it was just the two of them. Well, the film, lighting, wardrobe, and makeup crew were all still there too.

But Lucas only had eyes for Meg.

Seb came over with a blue velvet ring box and handed it to Lucas. Inside sat the biggest, gaudiest ring he'd ever seen. It was costume jewelry designed to make a statement. And it was awful.

"Seb, we can't use this."

"It will look great on camera," the director insisted.

But Lucas didn't care how great it might look in the video. This wasn't a ring he could ever imagine offering to Meg. "Meg, would you mind giving us your opinion on the engagement ring?"

She was silent for several seconds as she studied it. "You know what? It's not actually about the ring." She looked at Lucas as she spoke. "It's about sharing a beautiful moment in the moonlight—and having a soul-deep connection. We don't even have to see the ring. We only need to see you popping the question, then opening the box, looking totally in love."

Lucas wanted nothing more than to pull her into his arms and tell her how he felt about her, regardless of the film crew watching them…or the fact that none of this was supposed to be real.

Seb looked pensive, before finally nodding. "You know what? I think you're right again, Meg." He slapped Lucas on the back. "Mark my words, this is going to be your best video yet."

"This really is going to be my best video by far," Lucas said to Meg. "All thanks to you."

Not only had she come up with so many of the ideas for the video—but as far as Lucas was concerned, this wasn't about the two of them *acting* like they were falling for each other.

He had fallen for Meg from the first moment he'd set eyes on her…and he just kept falling harder and harder with every moment they spent together.

More than ever, he wanted to tell her this, wanted her to know exactly how he felt. But Seb was calling for them to take their places.

"Is everyone ready? Action!"

Lucas and Meg walked along the beach together in the moonlight, their arms around each other's waists. And then he stepped back, reached into his pocket for the ring box, and got down on one knee.

He paused to take in her radiant beauty. She was the one he'd been waiting for, everything he wanted. He opened the ring box. "Will you marry me?"

Meg didn't even look at the ring as she stared into his eyes, her gaze so full of emotion, more than he'd ever dreamed she could feel for him. He held his breath as he waited for her response.

Finally, she whispered, *"Yes."*

In one smooth move, he stood and swept her into his arms, twirling her around in a burst of sheer joy with the stars spinning in the night sky above them and the waves crashing against the shore in the background.

Meg felt so right in his arms that Lucas didn't stop to think, didn't hesitate this time, before lowering his mouth to hers.

She gasped softly against his lips, and then she was kissing him back passionately.

He couldn't get over how sweet she tasted, how good she felt pressed against him. He wanted to keep kissing her forever—

"Cut! Amazing!" Seb's voice broke the spell.

Meg didn't jump out of Lucas's arms at the interruption, simply drew back, looking a little confused. More than anything, he hoped he wasn't the only one who had forgotten it wasn't a real proposal.

"I can't believe we got nearly everything we needed in one take!" Seb enthused. "You two are on fire."

Lucas was still reeling from the incredible kiss, which had been so much more than just physical. It had been about their emotional connection, one that was so much deeper than he'd ever felt with anyone else.

Tuning out his director, he said in a low voice to Meg, "It felt right, didn't it?" Again, he held his breath as he waited for her response.

She lifted her hand to touch her lips for a brief moment. "It felt perfect."

Lucas knew they needed to talk about what had just happened. What their kiss meant. Because he needed to make it clear that, to him, it hadn't just been acting for a video. Their kiss had meant *everything*.

"Meg—"

"Okay, Lucas," Seb called, "I'm going to need you by yourself for a few more shots."

Lucas barely kept from growling, "I thought you said you got everything you needed."

"*Almost* everything. We still need shots of you with the ring box in the moonlight before the clouds shift and make continuity difficult during editing. And then another with you singing along to your track on the beach in case we want to splice some of that in." Seb turned to Meg. "You were great today. We've got an early start tomorrow, so you should probably head home and get some rest."

Lucas's heart fell at the prospect of Meg's leaving. He was tremendously frustrated at not being able to talk with her. He understood that they needed to get the final night shots for the video…but all he wanted was to finally tell Meg how he felt about her.

Unfortunately, she was already moving back, edging away with a look on her face that seemed to say she was rethinking the wisdom of their spontaneous kiss.

He stepped forward, ready to do or say whatever he could to take away her uncertainty.

But she was already turning away from him and saying, "I'll see you in the morning, Lucas. Good luck with the rest of the shoot tonight."

And then she was gone.

Chapter Ten

Today was the day Meg Ashworth married Lucas Crosby.

No, she reminded herself, today was the day she *played the part* of his bride.

After the kiss they'd shared the night before, it had been nearly impossible to remember that they were just acting for a music video. Especially now that Meg could no longer hide from the truth.

She was head over heels for him.

All this time, she'd cautioned herself not to make the mistake of falling for him. But how could she possibly resist when he was so sweet and kind and talented…and when his kiss had filled her with such deep desire?

It didn't help to find several messages waiting from her mother when she finally returned home and had a chance to turn on her cell phone for the first time all day. Meg's mother was, to put it mildly, *furious* that she had been a no-show for dinner.

Meg couldn't believe she had forgotten to get back

to her mother about not being able to attend dinner. It was just that things with Lucas and his video shoot were such a whirlwind, and he'd been all she could think about.

Once she'd returned home last night, after such a long day of filming, Meg hadn't had the energy to deal with her mother. Even sending a text, she knew, would be akin to poking an angry bear. While climbing into bed, she had sleepily vowed to get in touch with her mother the next day to explain. After filming, of course, given that she didn't want anything to disrupt her focus on Lucas's project until they were done.

By the time Meg arrived at Married in Malibu, Travis was busy herding the crew and extras into their designated areas, while working hard to keep the paparazzi—who had finally gotten wind of the video—out of the venue.

Meg's co-workers had done a wonderful job of transforming the hall during the last couple of days, turning it into a beautifully classic chapel. The flowers were gloriously in bloom, the three-tiered cake was breathtaking, and Amy had transformed the walls with paint so that they looked like stone.

The extras looked like a real wedding party in their suits and dresses. Some sipped apple cider in lieu of champagne, given that they were heading into a long day of filming. Others nibbled on Jenn's pastries and drank coffee from Tamara's café across the street.

At the heart of it all stood Lucas, dressed in a formal three-piece wedding suit.

When he saw her, he smiled and came toward her. "I've really been looking forward this morning to seeing you again."

Meg opened her mouth to reply, but she wasn't sure what to say. How could she, when she still had no idea whether Lucas's kiss had simply been acting…or if he'd kissed her because he was falling for her too?

"I've been looking forward to seeing you too," she said softly.

She couldn't quite meet his eyes, not when she was sure that if she did, he'd see everything she was feeling. The last thing she wanted was to put him in an uncomfortable position where he felt she was acting like one of his groupies, rather than his colleague.

He moved closer, taking her hands. "Meg—" He waited until she lifted her gaze to his. "I don't want to do anything that's going to make you unhappy. If something's wrong, you can tell me."

She thought she had mastered the art of not letting her emotions show. How could he see through her so easily?

"No, really, I'm a bit nervous about getting it all right today." That was the safest plan. Deflect everything she was feeling into work. Pretend everything was okay, the way she always had before. "We've got so much to get through—the wedding, the cake cutting, the first dance..."

And their next on-camera kiss.

"In fact," she added, desperate to move away before she did something crazy like beg him for another kiss, "I should probably get into the dress."

"You're going to be amazing," Lucas said in an encouraging voice. "But as soon as we get a break, we need to talk. I had hoped we could talk privately last night, but with the film crew needing the moonlight shots..." His frustration shone through. "Promise me we'll find a moment alone today."

She stared at him for a long moment before nodding. "Okay."

We need to talk never meant anything good. Most likely, it meant one of the following:

It's not you, it's me.

I hope I haven't given you the wrong idea.

It's been fun while it lasted—now go have a nice life without me.

Her gut churned as she realized he must have guessed the way she felt about him. Knowing Lucas, he was planning to let her down gently. Sit her down somewhere quiet, make sure that she was comfortable...and then tell her that he didn't feel the same way she did. He'd put it nicely—Meg couldn't imagine Lucas being anything other than kind or considerate. But he'd still talk about how they were very different people. And maybe how he was always on the road and couldn't sustain a relationship with anyone, let alone her.

Ultimately, it would all come down to one thing: They were never going to be together, because he would never see her as more than just a colleague or a friend.

Liz was waiting for her in the dressing room. She held out the beautiful gown. "What do you think?"

The wedding dress was incredible, a flowing net of lacework set over shimmering white silk, with discreet pastel sequins at the sleeves and hem giving flashes of color.

"It's…" She had to work very hard to keep from crying. "It's perfect."

Liz looked at her with concern. "Are you all right?"

Again, she'd let too much show on her face. What had happened to the days when she'd been so good at hiding her feelings that no one had been able to see behind the polite façade?

Or maybe it was simply that the people she used to spend time with hadn't cared enough about her to look that deeply.

"I'm fine," Meg insisted. "If you wouldn't mind helping me into the dress, I'm pretty sure Seb will be calling for me soon."

The dress fit her like a glove. There were actual gloves too, fingerless lace that turned her gown just a little bit rock 'n' roll.

Meg sat down at the dressing table to fix her hair and makeup—she'd already told the crew that she would take care of it herself this morning—but after a few minutes of trying to tame her hair into perfect submission, Liz gently brushed her hands away, taking over with the expertise that came from making last-minute adjustments for so many real brides.

"I heard yesterday's filming went really well," Liz said as she worked. She seemed to be unpicking a lot of the careful tidiness Meg had been aiming for.

"The director certainly seemed happy," Meg said.

"Well, I'm not surprised at all. You're incredibly good at your job."

That was always good to hear, especially coming from Liz. "Thank you."

"Having said that, I never guessed that you would end up starring in Lucas's video." Liz made a final adjustment, then gave a satisfied nod before dropping her hands to her sides.

The hairstyle was the opposite of anything Meg might have tried, with a windswept, day-at-the-beach feel to it. She couldn't imagine any bride actually walking down the aisle looking like this …

And yet it was just right.

Exactly the way Meg would have wanted to look on her real wedding day.

"You've gone above and beyond with this project," Liz said.

"It's not a problem," Meg assured her automatically.

Liz shook her head. "No, I'm serious. You've gone a million miles beyond anything we could reasonably expect of you. Your job is to design celebrity weddings, and here we've pushed you into a rock video. Rose, RJ, and I all want you to know how much we appreciate everything you've been doing. How much we appreciate *you*. And you shouldn't feel you have to do this to prove anything to us. If there are any parts of this that you're uncomfortable with, like the kiss I heard you shot last night in the cove, all you have to do is tell me and I'll step in."

"Lucas hasn't done anything to make me feel uncomfortable," Meg assured her. "I'm not saying this hasn't pushed me out of my comfort zone, because we all know it has. But I can make it through one more day of shooting."

"Are you absolutely sure?"

Saying anything else would tear the whole video apart. They'd already shot the bulk of the scenes, and there wouldn't be time to shoot them again with another bride. It meant a great deal to Meg to know that Liz was willing to turn the whole thing on its head if her employee wasn't happy, but Meg couldn't do it.

Besides, Lucas Crosby was waiting for her at the altar.

Which meant she'd get to kiss him one last time.

Meg looked her boss in the eye. "I'm sure."

* * *

Pausing at the top of the aisle, Meg took in the wedding scene.

Travis stood by the doors, his eagle eye on the crew, actors, and the entrance to the hall. Nate was running the lighting rig, while Daniel had his camera at the ready. Jenn stood beside her cake, ready to reapply new frosting if necessary beneath the hot lights. Kate was spritzing the blooms. Liz had her tablet in hand and headset on, like always. In addition to the Married in Malibu staff, Meg could see the cameras and the extras in place as wedding guests.

And yet…it all felt so real.

Had the extras been told to look at her with awe on their faces, as if a radiant bride had actually appeared?

And had Seb told Lucas to look a little nervous? As he followed her every move, she could see him swallow hard, his eyes full of wonder.

A gentle tug on her arm from the extra playing her father reminded Meg that they were waiting for her to walk down the aisle.

But as she began to glide forward, the dozens of strangers watching her, and the cameras, all ceased to matter. The only person who mattered was Lucas.

He looked like he was barely holding himself back from running to her. And when his best man tried to stop him, he pulled free with such force that even Meg found herself convinced that he truly was desperate to be close to her.

The next thing she knew, she was in his arms and he was spinning her in a circle, his hands strong around her waist as her dress fluttered against her legs. When he finally set her down, he held out his arm, and they walked together to the altar, where the officiant was waiting.

Her heart was pounding hard and fast as they made their way through an abbreviated wedding, as this was only about capturing a few seconds of film while the song played over the scene.

But even though no one would hear what they said, the actor playing the officiant asked, "Do you, Meg, take Lucas to be your husband?"

She felt breathless as she looked into Lucas's eyes. "I do."

"Do you, Lucas, take Meg to be your wife?"

Lucas's hands tightened over hers. "I do."

They exchanged rings next, classic platinum bands. Meg relished his touch, his strength, as she moved the band into place on his ring finger. For his part, he slid her ring onto her finger so delicately that thrill bumps moved over the surface of her skin.

The officiant said, "If anyone has any reason why these two should not be married..." After a short pause, the words she'd been dreading—and eagerly anticipating—came.

"I now pronounce you husband and wife. You may kiss the bride."

This kiss wasn't spontaneous, wasn't unplanned like their kiss on the beach. Meg had known it was coming. And yet...nothing she had imagined could ever have been enough to capture the sweet sensation of Lucas's hands whispering up her arms, to her shoulders, to drift, feather-light, over her cheek.

Only then did his lips press against hers.

His kiss was as gentle as his touch, and as intensely intimate. Meg couldn't keep herself from melting against him and kissing him back with all the love in her heart.

"Cut! That's great!" Seb called out. "Let's do it again, just like that."

Even with the director interrupting their kiss, it took Meg several seconds to draw back from Lucas. He seemed just as lost in the moment, both of them blinking at each other as though they weren't sure how they'd gone from sharing a sinfully sweet private moment to standing in the middle of a video shoot.

She came back to reality a beat before Lucas did, forcing herself to step away and make her way back up the aisle to shoot the scene again.

"Wait," Seb called. "You forgot the rings."

Meg looked down at her hand. It had just seemed so natural to wear Lucas's ring...and she'd been so stunned by the aftermath of the kiss that it had been hard to think clearly about anything at all.

Reluctantly, she took off the ring and gave it to the props person to set it back in its box.

As they ran through the scene again, and again, each time her walk down the aisle and the vows felt like nothing more than a prelude to the moment when Lucas kissed her, soft as a breath of air, washing over her like the tide. With every take, she couldn't help losing herself in his kiss, wishing she and Lucas could stay like that forever. And every time Seb yelled, "Cut!" it felt like a betrayal—an intrusion of reality into her perfect fantasy.

"Okay," Seb said after their fifth take. "I think we have all the shots we need for this scene. Let's move on to cake cutting and the first dance."

But Lucas was shaking his head. "I want to try one small change on a final take."

He leaned in toward Meg, so close that she could feel his breath running across her ear. "I'm going to do the *other* kiss this time."

Their post *I do* kisses had been gentle, slow, sensual,

delicate. But the *other* kiss, the one they'd talked about the day they'd been brainstorming this scene, was intended to be so passionate that it swept her off her feet.

Meg struggled to keep her composure as Seb agreed to do one more take. But her hands trembled as she slid the ring onto Lucas's finger, and by the time he returned the favor, she could barely breathe from the heady anticipation of what was about to happen.

"If anyone has any reason why these two should not be married..."

Into the pause came the sound of a commotion. When Meg realized someone was storming into the hall, her first thought was amazement that someone had managed to get past Travis.

Until she saw who it was...and then it didn't seem quite so amazing anymore.

Standing in the aisle, Meg's mother looked so severe that an army couldn't have stopped her from barging in.

"What on earth do you think *you* are doing with my daughter?" Judith Ashworth looked furious enough to breathe fire as she pointed at Lucas. "Take your hands off her *at once*!"

Chapter Eleven

Meg's mother was indomitable. The head of a dozen committees and the undisputed doyenne of Bel Air's high society, she was the kind of woman who would walk into a video shoot and expect it to stop for her.

But then, Meg had turned out to be very different from the way he'd expected someone from her world to be, hadn't she? Was there a chance that her mother could be too?

Lucas stepped forward, his hand outstretched. "Mrs. Ashworth, it's great to meet you. I'm Lucas Crosby."

She ignored his proffered right hand, instead concentrating on the wedding ring on his left.

Her mouth pinched as she turned to pin her steely gaze on her daughter. "I'll ask one more time, Margaret. What on *earth* is going on? Is this why you've been ignoring my calls? You've married *him*, and you didn't even tell me? Your own mother?"

"It's nothing like that, Mother." Meg's voice sounded smaller than usual. Less confident.

"Do you think I can't see what's going on here, Margaret? Honestly, I *knew* letting you work in a place like this would give you strange ideas. But getting married without so much as a by-your-leave? I have *never* been so disappointed in you."

Lucas stepped forward to defend her, but Meg put a hand on his arm. "Lucas is a musician." She gestured to the cameras. "This wedding is simply set up so that we can film a video for his new song."

Lucas could understand that it would be a shock to think that your daughter was getting married without telling you. But now that Mrs. Ashworth understood the real situation, surely she could relax enough for her and Meg to work things out between the two of them.

Wanting to help, he suggested, "Would you like a role in the video too, Mrs. Ashworth? It's probably a little late for you to give Meg away unless we reshoot the scene, but—"

"You actually think that *I* would agree to be involved in this…this video of yours? It's bad enough that you've persuaded my daughter to take part in this debacle." Her scorn crystal clear, she dismissed him again. "Margaret, I simply cannot believe what I am seeing here. How could you do this?"

"Mother, as I've explained, it's—"

"*Don't* interrupt," her mother scolded, even though she was the one interrupting. "You are bringing great shame on our family by pretending to be some tramp in a trashy music video with a man like *this*!"

"Don't talk about Lucas like that." Meg's words flashed out with surprising force. "Like he's somehow *less* than you are—when the truth is that he's worth far more than anyone in your world will ever be."

"Margaret Ashworth!" her mother snapped. "You are behaving like an ungrateful, spoiled brat!"

Enough was enough. "You can't speak to Meg like that," Lucas told her. "You owe your daughter an apology. *Now.*"

The gaze her mother turned on him was so furious, Lucas was surprised lightning didn't strike him. Clearly, Meg's mother was not used to people talking back to her—or demanding an apology.

"I will speak to my daughter in whatever way I wish, without some *gutter rat* telling me how best to do it."

"Too bad, because I'm going to tell you whether you like it or not." He took a step closer to Meg's mother, his fury matching hers. "Do you have any idea how much effort your daughter has put into this video? Do you even realize just how great she is at what she does?"

"I don't need a lecture from *you* about the things my daughter chooses to do with her spare time."

"Spare time?" Lucas could hardly believe what he was hearing. "This is Meg's *job*. It's what she does for a living, not some hobby."

"That's where you're wrong. She has no need of the money. Being a part of this—" Judith waved her hands dismissively at the hall and gardens. "—does not benefit a good cause. Therefore, it is nothing more than a hobby. And a worthless one at that."

Trying to reason with Meg's mother was like trying to reason with a brick wall. Hating that he hadn't yet been able to convince her to back down or apologize, he turned back to Meg to find tears glistening in her eyes. Her gloved hands had formed fists and she was shaking.

Wanting to shield her from further pain, he reached for her. But she stepped back before his hands could cover hers.

"You don't have to do this alone," Lucas said in a low voice. He didn't care how many people were watching them, or that the cameras, and camera phones, might still be rolling, for all he knew. He needed Meg to know how he felt about her—that he loved her, heart and soul.

But before he could, she said, "Mother, we should speak in private so that I can better explain the situation," and headed toward the exit.

Before she left the room, however, Meg took the ring off her finger and set it on the edge of one of the pews. After a moment's hesitation, she took off the gloves that went with her dress too, leaving them behind.

Lucas was desperate to follow them. To be by Meg's side from this moment forward and support her in any way he could.

But no matter how much he loved her, no matter how much he wanted to be a part of her life, he couldn't force himself into it if she didn't want him there.

The truth he didn't like having to face was that he wasn't her husband anywhere but in the fantasy of his music video.

Walking over to where she'd set her ring, he settled it on his pinky so that it wouldn't go missing, then sat down in the empty pew. For once, everyone kept their distance.

* * *

Still in her beautiful wedding gown, Meg led her mother up to her office, letting her in among the color charts and fabric samples. Until this week, she would have said it was the place in the world where she felt safest—but then Lucas had held her, and she realized she felt safest in his arms.

"This tiny little room is where you…work?" her mother said. She made *work* sound like a dirty word.

"This is my office, yes." It wouldn't have taken much effort for her mother to visit her office before now. And yet, she never had. "I'm surprised to see you here today."

"I had no intention of ever setting foot in this place. Bu you haven't replied to my texts. You haven't called. You didn't come to dinner. And you haven't shown up for the meetings I've scheduled."

"I'm sorry I haven't had a chance to call you back sooner, but I told you earlier in the week that I had to work," Meg reminded her.

"Gallivanting around with some *musician* isn't work." Her mother's eagle eye took in everything in Meg's office that was half finished and messy. "When you told me that you would be working with celebrities, that was bad enough, but this video nonsense is simply too much."

"I know you're disappointed—"

"*Disappointed* is hardly the word." She wouldn't have used that harsh of a tone even if one of the household staff had dropped a priceless vase on the marble floor. "You're cavorting with extremely undesirable types who are probably all on drugs."

"Lucas isn't on drugs."

"If it isn't drugs, it will be *something*. These are not our kind of people."

Meg hated everything about her mother's statement. "You're wrong."

But it was as if her mother hadn't heard. "What did you think you were doing, agreeing to take part in this filth?"

Meg knew how arguments with her mother went, and not a single one had ever ended with her winning. Judith Ashworth didn't understand the concept of giving in.

But this time, Meg had to protest, "It's nothing like that. The video is actually rather sweet. I helped to design it."

If she'd been hoping that might spark some hint of parental pride, it was a forlorn hope.

"Do you think I was born yesterday? Do you think I don't know that music videos are full of half-naked women and obscene lyrics? It's disgusting and *completely* unacceptable for the management to force you into taking part in such a thing."

"Nobody forced me into anything."

Again, her mother didn't seem to be listening as she walked behind the desk and sat in Meg's chair. "It's obvious that you're letting these people push you around too much. And just look at the results—you've hardly done a thing for my charity dinner all week."

Meg wanted to point out that she'd never signed up to do it at all. That she'd only agreed to come up with a few ideas. But her mother was still talking.

"Surely nothing you're doing here is as important as the good works the foundation will do. All you've done this week is play around in a video that is going to be social *death* if anyone we know sees it. I wouldn't be able to live with the shame if anyone mentioned it at a dinner party."

"I don't think anyone you know watches rock videos," Meg said. If she'd been feeling more confident, she might have been able to make a joke, rather than the words coming out sounding like an excuse.

"No, they certainly do not," her mother agreed. "And with good reason. Obviously, your foolish infatuation with that musician has overridden your common sense."

"I don't... I'm not..."

"Stop dithering, Margaret. I was only in the room for a few minutes, and even I could see the way you looked at him."

"It was just acting," Meg tried.

"Don't lie to me. You're my daughter. I know you better than anyone."

Once upon a time, Meg would have believed that was true. But her mother saw only the parts of her that she wanted to see, banishing everything else behind the rules of propriety.

"This is the day when you stop your nonsense once and for all," her mother continued. "After you change out of that ridiculous dress, you will be coming home with me. It's time you remembered what is truly important in life. Family. Duty." She waved her hand at Meg to hurry her into action. "Get out of that and fetch your things. And be quick. I've left my driver waiting."

Meg felt as though they were having an instant replay of a conversation from several weeks earlier. She had been summoned to her mother's for tea, and when she'd casually mentioned that Lucas would be filming a video at Married in Malibu, her mother had insisted she quit her job. That day, it had taken everything in Meg to go against a lifetime of the *duty* her mother spoke of and say no.

Having done it before, it should have been easier now. How she wished that were the case as she forced the word from her lips. "No."

Her mother raised a perfectly plucked eyebrow. "Excuse me?"

Though Meg hated having such a bitter confrontation, the one thing her mother had left off her list of what was truly important in life—*love*—drove Meg forward. "I have to finish filming the video."

Her mother's eyes were wide with disbelief. "After everything I've just said, you're going to disobey me?"

"I gave my word that I would do this, and I'm going to follow through with it."

"Even if it means abandoning your own mother?" Judith said it as though she were frail and fragile, rather than a force of nature backed by extreme wealth and a dozen household staff.

"I'm not abandoning you," Meg said in as gentle a

voice as she could manage. "But the truth you need to recognize is that I have a job and a life that I can't just drop every time you call. Tomorrow afternoon, I'll come by to help you."

Her mother stood perfectly still for several seconds, obviously trying to process the idea that her dutiful daughter had failed to do as she wished. "If you go back in there, Margaret, and take part in that video, then you are *not* the daughter I thought I had raised."

"I'm sorry you feel that way." It took everything she had to head for the door to return to the video shoot. Not doing so would mean breaking her promise to Lucas. And she would never hurt him like that, no matter the cost to herself. "I'll see you tomorrow."

Her legs were shaking as she walked back downstairs, but thankfully she had years of poise and comportment lessons to draw on. It was going to be difficult to jump back into the video shoot after her mother's jarring interruption. Difficult to hide her sorrow over having alienated, and possibly even losing, her mother…

And most of all, nearly impossible to hide her love for the rock star she hadn't been able to resist from the first moment he'd made her laugh in the middle of a crowded room.

Chapter Twelve

Lucas waited anxiously by the door for Meg to return. Her mother had said so many hurtful things in public—he could only imagine how harsh she might be in private.

Meg's face was a careful mask as she walked in. Lucas had thought he'd succeeded in pulling that mask away over the course of the week. Now, here it was again, thicker than ever.

"Are you okay? What happened? What did your mother say to you?"

Instead of answering, Meg simply shook her head.

"We don't need to continue filming." He reached for her hands, which were ice cold. "We can shut everything down and—"

"No." She took a breath and held it for a moment, before saying, "I want to keep filming."

"Meg, it's okay. You don't have to do this."

At last, her shoulders went back and fire returned to her gaze. "I *want* to do this."

Lucas loved how strong she was in the face of everything her mother must have thrown at her. He loved her determination, her focus on making things better for everyone around her. But he hated knowing he was responsible for her current problems.

He'd pushed her out of her comfort zone by begging her to star in his video. He'd kissed her again and again, with fierce passion that was a million miles from the actor's screen kiss she'd thought she was signing up for when she'd agreed to do this. And then he'd made things even worse by arguing—in public—with her mother.

"Meg!" Seb called from across the room. "Are you done dealing with your family issues so that we can film?" The director had absolutely no tact, but compared to Meg's mom, he now seemed gentle as a lamb.

"Yes, I'm ready." This time when she spoke, her voice was clear and strong.

"Good. After that long interruption, we're going to miss the sunset for the final scene if we film that extra take, Lucas. We're going to have to skip that and go straight into the first dance, then the cake cutting, then the two of you driving away in the convertible." The dance floor had already been set up, so Seb motioned for the crew and cast to quickly take their places.

"Are you sure you're okay to do this?" Lucas had to ask again. "Just say the word and we'll stop."

"And throw away your whole video?" Meg shook

her head. "There's no way I'm going to let all this work go to waste. I can do this. I'm fine."

Lucas could see that she was anything but fine, but he couldn't insist that they stop when she was putting so much effort into completing what they'd started. She was so strong. And he'd never loved anyone more.

Thank God they were filming the first dance, because that meant he could give in to his longing to pull her into his arms.

As they danced, he drank in every sweet sensation—her body moving with his, her delicate scent, the heat of her skin against his. But whenever she seemed about to lose herself in their dance, she quickly put a small space between them, almost as though she was afraid to have too much contact with him.

"Two more scenes, people!" Seb called as soon as he was happy with their dance, ushering everyone over to the three-tiered cake. "Remember, we don't have a backup cake, so you two have got to nail this in one take."

Meg picked up the cake knife, then Lucas stepped behind her, wrapping his hands over hers, relishing her closeness. Together, they brought the knife down on the first layer of the cake, slicing through it easily.

He never wanted to let her go, not even enough to feed each other the ceremonial bites of cake. But this was their only take, so he couldn't screw it up.

Too soon, Meg was surrounded by hair and makeup people to get her ready for their final scene in the convertible. Her friend Kate was there as well, to give her a fresh bouquet to throw into the sky as they were driving away.

He hoped that while they were alone in the front seat of the car, he'd have a chance to talk to her. But for this final scene, there were more crew members than ever around them, making sure the lighting and positioning of the car were exactly right so that they could nail the shot just as the sun set over the ocean.

Filming the final scene seemed to happen in a blur. They took their places in the car, Lucas turned on the ignition and started driving, then Seb yelled for Meg to throw the bouquet. They filmed the scene a half-dozen more times before the sun fell too low in the sky.

"And...cut!" Seb did a little dance in place. "That's a wrap!"

Just that quickly, Meg was out of the car and heading in the direction of the dressing rooms. She cut through the crowd of extras smoothly, while Lucas had to dodge everyone wanting a photograph or simply to congratulate him on a great song and video. Any other time, he would have taken the time to chat with everyone and thank them for helping with his video.

But he needed to talk with Meg before it was too late.

She was at the door to the bride's dressing room by the time he caught up to her. "Meg, wait. I need to talk to you."

"About what you were going to say before?" When he nodded, she held up her hand. "It's okay. You don't need to say anything. I understand."

"You do?"

"Of course I do. I know this was just a video shoot, nothing more."

"No, that wasn't what I was going to say. Not at all." The ferocity in his voice made her eyes widen. He moved forward and took her hands in his. "I've wanted to say this almost since I met you. I should have said it days ago." She was so beautiful, so sweet, so wonderful in every way. "I love you."

Meg stared at him in shock. "What? That's not… You can't…"

"I love you," Lucas repeated. "This hasn't been acting for me. None of it. Every time I've been pretending to fall in love with you for the video, the truth is that it's been *real* for me. I want to be with you, Meg—and I hope you want to be with me too."

She stared at him in silence, her eyes even wider now.

"Please say something."

Finally, she spoke. "I… I can't be with you. I can't be what you need me to be."

"You're already *everything* I need you to be."

But Meg was shaking her head and pulling her hands from his. "I'm not. You need someone who can fit into your world. Someone who doesn't come with my mother. If we were together, she'd be attacking you every minute of the day."

"It's not your mother I'm in love with."

"But she comes as part of the package. I am who I am, Lucas. I wish I could change for you, but—"

"I'm not asking you to be anyone else. I don't want you to change. And I'm not worried about your mom. We can make this work. We already are."

"In a video," Meg pointed out.

"Not just in the video." Lucas was desperate to make her see. "We've been a perfect fit from the very start. We make each other happier. We inspire each other. I've felt it every moment we've been together."

"I'm sorry." Her eyes were glassy with unshed tears. "I'll never be able to fit into your world. Our lives are just too different."

Lucas reached out to take her hands again, praying she'd feel their connection. "You could be a part of any world you wanted. And I will do anything it takes to fit into yours."

He could see her reluctance to pull away. But she made herself do it anyway.

"I'm sorry." She stepped into the dressing room.

And as the door swung shut behind her, the last glimpse Lucas had of her face was a picture of absolute heartbreak.

Chapter Thirteen

Judith Ashworth's house had never felt particularly welcoming, but by the time Meg finally felt ready to face her mother late the next afternoon, just as the sun was beginning to set, it was positively forbidding. Even Bertrand, the butler who answered the door, barely made eye contact. All he said was, "Mrs. Ashworth is waiting for you in the conservatory."

Normally, Meg's journey through the house was like walking through a museum. Now, it felt like a trip to the executioner's block.

The conservatory had a view that was the best money could buy. Papers and designs relating to the charity dinner surrounded her mother like props meant to remind Meg of the responsibilities she'd ignored.

"There you are, Margaret." Her mother didn't hide her victorious tone. "Come sit, there is a lot of work to be done."

Meg stopped in her tracks. "Aren't we going to discuss what happened yesterday?"

"We have far too much work to do."

She had expected her mother to demand an apology, at the very least. But that wasn't the way their family did things, was it?

Don't talk about anything.

Take your victories where you can.

Pretend that everything is fine and hide even the largest problems with a fine layer of civility.

On autopilot, Meg sat and began to go through the arrangements for the dinner, shifting the seating plan and adjusting the calligraphy on the menu, while her mother chattered about who was in and out of favor this week.

"...of course, Ellen insisted the funding should go through her badly run foundation..."

"...if rumors can be believed, James and his new bride are off to Bolivia for their honeymoon. Bolivia! I can't imagine what they must be thinking to forgo the wonders of Europe..."

"...couldn't believe my eyes when I saw Candice wearing last year's off-the-rack..."

Meg had always told herself that she couldn't fault her mother for her gossip when she concentrated so much of her energy on charitable works. Today, however, she couldn't get herself to believe it.

"Mother—"

"Don't interrupt, Margaret."

"Are we really not going to talk about what happened yesterday?" She waited until she was sure that she had her mother's full attention. "Are you really going to sit here and talk about a bunch of random people rather than try to work through our differences?"

"What is there to talk about? Obviously, you're here because you have finally come to your senses and put your silly dalliance with that rock star behind you."

"I'm here because I promised I would help you with these plans, not because of any *dalliance*," Meg corrected her.

"It's hardly enough, though, is it? This business with the musician—" Her mother's mouth puckered as though she'd been sucking on a lemon. "—is a symptom, rather than the disease itself."

"A symptom?" Meg said. "Is that how you see me? As diseased?"

"Well, there's certainly *something* wrong with you. You would never have spoken to me like this a few months ago."

"That's true," Meg said slowly. She would never have dared to talk back to her before she started working at Married in Malibu. Probably because working alongside her supportive friends had shown her that she could do something worthwhile. Something more than simply following her mother's instructions.

And Lucas...

Lucas had shown her so much more than that. His deeply heartfelt *I love you* was playing inside her head when her mother spoke again.

"As I was saying, you've gone too far. That scene yesterday was simply the pinnacle of it all. I thought that if I gave you some time, you would work through this phase and realize what is truly important. But it seems that you aren't going to come out of it without my guidance."

Guidance? That's what her mother called delivering an ultimatum in the middle of Meg's workplace—and then deliberately ignoring the deep fractures in their relationship?

"After everything you've done, I'm *dying* to hear what additional guidance you could possibly have for me." Though Meg had said no to her mother a few times recently, she hadn't ever had the courage to get this angry with her, let alone express it. But now she couldn't seem to stop herself.

"Watch your tone with me, Margaret. I am still your mother!"

That was what it always came back to, wasn't it? Relying on *family* to force Meg to do what she wanted. Using *family* as an excuse for treating Meg as badly she wanted to. Her mother didn't have to be kind, or respect Meg's own dreams and desires, because they were *family*.

But it wasn't the whole family that came first. It was Judith Ashworth—with Meg a long, long way down the list.

"It is obvious where your sudden rebellion has come from. Well, that stops now."

"Excuse me?" Meg could sound just as imperious as her mother. After all, she'd learned from the very best. Besides, how many times did her mother expect them to go around and around on this subject? Until Meg finally broke down and acquiesced?

"I should think my meaning is clear enough. It's long past time to quit this job of yours and forget all of this nonsense completely. I'm your mother and I know what's best for you."

"I've spent my life believing that," Meg said in a low voice, "but I've finally realized that the only person you want the best for is *you*."

"I'm simply looking out for your well-being," her mother insisted.

"I'd like to believe that—" And the truth was that she really did. "But I honestly don't think you know how."

Shock flashed across her mother's features, swiftly followed by fury. "Do you have any idea how embarrassed you will be when that video comes out and people start gossiping about you?"

"The only person who is going to feel embarrassed is you. I certainly won't, because I have nothing whatsoever to feel embarrassed about. I'm proud of what I do. I'm proud of my job. I'm proud that I help give people the weddings they've always dreamed of. And I have every intention of continuing to do just that."

"I would think very carefully about your next actions, Margaret. Because if you don't give up this silliness at once, there simply won't be a place for you here anymore."

This was where Meg would have folded before, the line in the sand she'd always been terrified to cross.

But this time, the wave of panic didn't come. Okay, so maybe the panic wasn't completely gone, but it was a smaller wave, at least. A ripple. Because this time, Meg knew that she had plenty of lifelines outside of her mother. She had friends.

And maybe even a man to love who loved her right back.

"Obviously," she said in a voice that surprised her by its steadiness, "you think I'm the one who should be afraid if we don't see one another. But I've finally realized that *you're* the one who needs *me*. I think..." It was important to stay strong, no matter how difficult this was to say. "I think we should take a break from one another for a while."

"A break?" Her mother looked utterly shocked. "You can't take a break from your own *mother*."

"Actually," Meg said in a soft but firm voice, "I can.

I'm going to give you some time to decide whether you're willing to love me for who I am...or if you can only love the person you want me to be."

"What is that supposed to mean?" her mother demanded.

Meg stood up. "It means that I'm leaving."

"And abandoning your responsibilities?" Her mother made another gesture toward the table. "What about the dinner?"

"You can hire someone to do that for you," Meg said. "Or you could do it yourself."

With that, she left the conservatory and headed back through the house. She had just opened the front door and was about to step outside, when she heard the rapid click of expensive heels.

"Come back here this minute!" Her mother was red in the face. "And don't you dare act like you can't hear me, Margaret."

"I can hear you just fine," she replied. "Just as I know you heard me perfectly well when I explained why we're taking a break." She was about to close the door behind her, when she turned back to say one more thing. "And when we do begin to mend our fences, I would appreciate it if you would use the name I prefer to go by now—*Meg*."

⋆ ⋆ ⋆

By the time Meg let herself into her apartment half an hour later, she had never felt so exhausted—or so wired at the same time.

More than once, she picked up her phone to contact Lucas. But she still felt so shaky.

Yes, she'd finally stood up to her mother. But did that mean she could reach for *everything* she truly wanted in her life—not only her dream job, but her dream man as well? Especially after she'd blown it so badly with him the day before, when he'd tried to tell her how he felt...

Pouring herself a glass of wine that she hoped would ease her nerves, she turned on Rachmaninoff. But the classical music that used to relax her didn't sound right tonight. Impulsively, she went online to hunt for music by the band she and Lucas had seen together at The Satellite.

As soon as she hit *Play*, memories came flooding back. Not only of the night they'd gone to the gig, but also every moment they'd shared. Telling each other about their childhoods and where they'd grown up. The way they'd laughed together while feeding the penguins. Their first kiss on the beach. Saying *I do* for his video, then cutting the cake together with his arms wrapped around her and his hand over hers. Then driving off into the sunset, the wind whipping through her hair as she threw the bouquet into the sky.

When a knock came at her door, she literally jumped

off the couch.

Could it be Lucas?

But when she opened the door, her next-door neighbor was standing on the mat, a small box in her hand. "This package was accidentally delivered to me."

Meg recognized the handwriting. What could Lucas have sent her?

Inside the box was a blue thumb drive and a note.

I asked Seb to put together this rough cut for you. Let me know if you want to make changes, or if you think it's already perfect just the way it is.

Meg's heart was pounding so hard she could hear the blood rushing in her ears as she slid the drive into her computer. As soon as she did, "Perfect Moments" began to play. Her heart was in her throat as she saw herself onscreen with Lucas for the first time, when he'd made her laugh whispering into her ear. Next came glimpses of their dates, intercut with the proposal, the beginning of the wedding, the walk down the aisle. And then...their kiss.

It was amazing how the individual scenes came together so well as a single story. But as she played the video again, she realized that they had created more than just a visual backdrop for a song.

They'd written the story of a man and woman falling in love.

Not only in the video, but in real life.

Meg hadn't been acting when she'd shot those scenes. At last, she realized that Lucas had meant it when he said he hadn't been acting either.

Maybe the two of them—the rock star from the wrong side of the tracks and the society girl finally breaking out of her gilded cage—didn't make sense.

But wasn't it also true that for all those years that her life *had* made perfect sense, she hadn't been happy?

She reached for her phone and typed a message to Lucas.

I don't want to change a thing. The video is perfect.

And so are we.

She was just about to send it when another knock came at her door. Was there more to the delivery than this one package?

She opened the door, expecting to see her neighbor again.

This time, Lucas was standing on the mat.

Only, instead of looking like the rock star she'd come to love so dearly over the past week, he was dressed like a banker in a three-piece suit, with his hair neatly cut, his chin smooth and stubble-free, and his tattoos covered.

"Lucas?" She could hardly believe he was here. Let alone looking like he'd just stepped out of the pages of a high-society magazine.

Wordlessly, she invited him in.

"I will do whatever it takes to fit into your world," he said before she could ask why he'd changed up his entire look. "I will change anything you need me to change."

"I would *never* want you to change who you are for me."

"I know you wouldn't, but I'm still going to do whatever it takes to win your heart. I'll do anything for you, Meg. Anything at all, if it means having your love."

"If you've watched the rough cut of the video," she said softly, "then you must know that you already do."

Hoped flared in his eyes. "Are you saying—"

"That I love you?" She put her hands on either side of his handsome face and gazed into his dark blue eyes. "I know it's coming a day too late, but yes, that's exactly what I'm saying. I love you, Lucas Crosby. I love you so very much."

"It could never be too late to hear you say that you love me. And I love you too, Meg Ashworth."

"Just promise me one thing," Meg said.

"Anything."

"That you'll always be you, no matter what anyone thinks, even me."

"As long as you promise me the same thing." He wrapped his arms around her and held her close. "I fell in love with you for exactly who you are—and no matter how you or I change and grow over the years, I vow that I will love you forever."

At last, they shared the sinfully passionate, and deeply loving, *forever* kiss that they'd both been longing for.

When they finally came up for air, her eyes were sparkling. "I thought the video was perfect, but now I realize there is one scene that isn't quite right." She relished the hit of wickedness that ran through her as she told him, "Instead of driving away in a convertible, we should have been on your motorcycle."

Surprise and anticipation lit his gaze. "It's outside if you want to take a ride with me tonight."

"I do," she said, kissing him again. "I definitely do."

And as Meg put on her leather jacket, walked hand in hand with Lucas to his Harley, and rode with him beneath the glow of the moonlight, she knew that this was just the start of the wild and crazy life she was bound to have with a rock star.

She grinned as she wrapped her arms tighter around his waist.

She couldn't wait.

Epilogue

Lucas and his record label held the launch party at a packed club. Nate had spent the past couple of hours setting up the feed to several big screens that would all play the "Perfect Moments" music video simultaneously. Now, as Lucas and his band took the stage, Meg stood beside him, looking radiantly happy.

Everyone from Married in Malibu was here tonight. Travis had his arm around Amy, although he kept shooting glances at the security team to make sure they were performing to his extremely high specifications. Liz was curled tight in Jason's arms. Jenn and Daniel were laughing together over a private joke. And Kate was standing with Tamara by the bar. Though Kate was wearing her usual outfit of jeans and a T-shirt, both were clean of soil smudges tonight. Tamara had rocked up her look for the evening, however. Not with denim and leather, but with floating layers à la Stevie Nicks or Kate Bush. She looked gorgeous, just like always.

It amazed Nate how so many of his friends had

found happiness and were settling down, after finding their true loves in the most unexpected places.

Lucas stepped up to the microphone. Taking Meg's hand, he brought her to his side. "This song goes out to everyone who has been lucky enough to find true love. But more than that, it's for Meg Ashworth, the woman *I* love. It's called 'Perfect Moments.'"

Pulling her close, Lucas kissed Meg. Her face was flushed and her eyes were bright as she took a few steps back into the wings of the stage as his band began playing the song live in perfect sync with the video.

Pleased to have another job successfully completed, Nate headed toward the bar.

"Where do you think you're going?" Tamara intercepted him halfway there. "Come and dance!"

Normally, Nate avoided dancing like the plague. After all, computer engineers and dance floors rarely mixed. But Tamara was so fun and sweet and alive that he couldn't resist her invitation.

All of the couples on the dance floor were moving close as the romantic song played, and in the crowd, it was natural for Nate to take Tamara into his arms.

Just as natural as it suddenly seemed to wonder what it might be like to kiss her.

* * * * *

For news on upcoming books, sign up for Lucy Kevin's New Release Newsletter

LucyKevin.com/Newsletter

ABOUT THE AUTHOR

Lucy Kevin is the pen name for Bella Andre. Having sold more than 8 million books, Bella Andre's novels have been #1 bestsellers around the world and have appeared on the *New York Times* and *USA Today* bestseller lists 85 times. She has been the #1 Ranked Author on a top 10 list that included Nora Roberts, JK Rowling, James Patterson and Steven King, and Publishers Weekly named Oak Press (the publishing company she created to publish her own books) the Fastest-Growing Independent Publisher in the US. After signing a groundbreaking 7-figure print-only deal with Harlequin MIRA, Bella's "The Sullivans" series has been released in paperback in the US, Canada, and Australia.

Known for "sensual, empowered stories enveloped in heady romance" (Publishers Weekly), her books have been Cosmopolitan Magazine "Red Hot Reads" twice and have been translated into ten languages. Winner of the Award of Excellence, The Washington Post called her "One of the top writers in America" and she has been featured by Entertainment Weekly, NPR, USA Today, Forbes, The Wall Street Journal, and TIME Magazine. A graduate of Stanford University, she has given keynote speeches at publishing conferences from Copenhagen to Berlin to San Francisco, including a standing-room-only keynote at Book Expo America in

New York City.

If not behind her computer, you can find her reading her favorite authors, hiking, swimming or laughing. Married with two children, Bella splits her time between the Northern California wine country, a 100 year old log cabin in the Adirondacks, and a flat in London overlooking the Thames.

For a complete listing of books, as well as excerpts and contests, and to connect with Bella:

Sign up for Lucy's newsletter:

lucykevin.com/newsletter

Visit Lucy's website at:

www.LucyKevin.com

Sign up for Bella's newsletter:

www.bellaandre.com/Newsletter

Visit Bella's website at:

www.BellaAndre.com

Follow Bella on Twitter at:

twitter.com/bellaandre

Join Bella on Facebook at:

facebook.com/bellaandrefans

Follow Bella on Instagram:

instagram.com/bellaandrebooks

Made in the USA
Middletown, DE
11 January 2019